THE
TOUR

Music and Lyrics by
JERRY HERMAN

Book by
MICHAEL STEWART & MARK BRAMBLE

**(Based on S. N. Behrman's adaptation
of Franz Werfel's play
Jacobowsky And The Colonel)**

SAMUEL FRENCH, INC.
25 WEST 45TH STREET   **NEW YORK 10036**
7623 SUNSET BOULEVARD   **HOLLYWOOD 90046**
LONDON   *TORONTO*

Amateurs wishing to arrange for the production of THE GRAND TOUR must make application to SAMUEL FRENCH, INC., at 25 West 45th Street, New York, N.Y. 10036, giving the following particulars:

(1) The name of the town and theatre or hall in which it is proposed to give the production.

(2) The maximum seating capacity of the theatre or hall.

(3) Scale of ticket prices.

(4) The number of performances it is intended to give, and the dates thereof.

(5) Indicate whether you will use an orchestration or simply a piano.

Upon receipt of these particulars SAMUEL FRENCH, INC., will quote the terms upon which permission for performances will be granted.

For all other rights apply to SAMUEL FRENCH, INC. N.Y. address only.

A set of orchestral parts consisting of: Reed I—flute, clarinet, piccolo; Reed II—oboe, tenor sax, English horn; Reed III—clarinet, bass clarinet; Reed IV—bassoon, flute, clarinet; Horns 1 & 2, Trumpets 1 & 2, Trombone, Violins ABC (3 books), Cello, Viola, Bass, Mandolin/Banjo, Accordion, Harp, Percussion (2 books), with piano conductor score will be loaned two months prior to the production ONLY on receipt of the royalty quoted for all performances, the rental fee and a refundable deposit. The deposit will be refunded on the safe return to SAMUEL FRENCH, INC. of all material loaned for the production.

Printed in U.S.A.

ISBN 0 573 68100

OPENING NIGHT JANUARY 11, 1979

THE PALACE THEATRE
UNDER THE DIRECTION OF THE MESSRS. NEDERLANDER

JAMES M. NEDERLANDER   DIANA SHUMLIN   JACK SCHLISSEL
in association with **CAROLE J. SHORENSTEIN** and **STEWART F. LANE**
present

JOEL GREY
in the musical

THE GRAND TOUR
Music and Lyrics by
JERRY HERMAN
Book by
MICHAEL STEWART *and* MARK BRAMBLE
based upon the original play JACOBOWSKY AND THE COLONEL
by Franz Werfel
and the American play based on the same by S. N. Behrman
Also Starring
RON HOLGATE
with

STEPHEN VINOVICH   GEORGE REINHOLT   GENE VARRONE   CHEVI COLTON
GRACE KEAGY   TRAVIS HUDSON   JAY STUART
and
FLORENCE LACEY

Sets by	*Costumes by*	*Lighting by*
MING CHO LEE	**THEONI V. ALDREDGE**	**MARTIN ARONSTEIN**

Dance Music

Musical Direction	*Orchestrations*	*Arranged by*	*Vocal Arrangements*
WALLY HARPER	**PHILIP J. LANG**	**PETER HOWARD**	**DONALD PIPPIN**

Assistant Choreographer	*Hair Designs & Makeup by*
MERCEDES ELLINGTON	**VINCENZO PRESTIA**

Choreography by
DONALD SADDLER
Directed by
GERALD FREEDMAN

Original cast album on Columbia records and tapes

CAST OF THE BROADWAY PRODUCTION
(*in order of appearance*)

S. L. Jacobowsky	Joel Grey
Mme. Bouffier	Grace Keagy
Cziesno	Jack Karcher
Jeannot	Mark Waldrop
Colonel Tadeusz Boleslav Stjerbinsky	Ron Holgate
Szabuniewicz	Stephen Vinovich
Chauffeur	Stan Page
Captain Meuller	George Reinholt
Mme. Vauclain	Chevi Colton
Marianne	Florence Lacey
Conductor	Gene Varrone
Mme. Marville an Elegant Lady	Travis Hudson
A Peasant Woman	Grace Keagy
Hugo the Hungarian Hercules	Kenneth Kantor
Mme. Manzoni	Chevi Colton
Stiltwalker	Jay Pierce
Bargeman	Kenneth Kantor
Man with Flower in His Lapel	Jay Stuart
Papa Clairon	Jay Pierce
Claudine	Jo Speros
Bride's Mother	Grace Keagy
Bride's Father	Gene Varrone
Bride's Aunt	Chevi Colton
Groom	Mark Waldrop
Bride	Michelle Marshall
Commissaire of Police	Bob Morrisey
Peddler	Stan Page
Mother Madeleine	Travis Hudson
Sister Roland	Grace Keagy

Refugees, Parisians, Train Travelers, Carnival Performers, German Soldiers, Wedding Guests, Sisters of Charity ......
Bjarne Buchtrup, Carol Dorian, Kenneth Kantor, Jack Karcher, Debra Lyman, Michelle Marshall, Bob Morrisey, Stan Page, Tina Paul, Jay Pierce, Linda Poser, Theresa Rakov, Paul Solen, Jo Speros, Mark Waldrop, Jeff Veazey, Bonnie Young

SWING DANCERS
Bronna Lipton, Jeff Richards

4

DESCRIPTION OF CHARACTERS

JACOBOWSKY—He is a "small man" wearing a well-cut suit, bought in happier days, which has managed to retain an air of elegance even though it is somewhat shiny. He has a neat bow tie, a neat voice and everything about him has the crisp edge of tidiness. You feel that in the lives he has been forced to migrate from everything was in good order; that his extra shoes had a good polish; his correspondence was caught up; his desk clear and that when people crossed the threshold of his house to come to dinner they felt a glow of benevolence and the quickened anticipation of a happy evening. His cheerfulness is an emanation from a harried past; he knows that the worst will probably happen, so that your only chance to improve the immediate present. This he is constantly trying to do in every small relation of life. He likes people and he wants them, if it is at all possible, to like him.

COLONEL—He is magnificent in his uniform, tall, commanding, aristocratic, electric with vitality, euphoric with a sense of his own immemorial authority in the scheme of things.

SZABUNIEWICZ—The COLONEL's orderly, Polish open-faced, sunny natured comedian, he is totally devoted to the COLONEL.

MARIANNE—A very lovely and vivacious Frenchwoman, in her late twenties, decidedly a woman and not a girl.

CAPTAIN MEULLER—S.S. Captain, suave, sharp, and menacing.

MME. BOUFFIER—Warm, late fifties, owner of a second class Paris hotel, and friend to Jacobowsky.

MME. MANZONI—Middle-aged owner of a small travelling circus. Flamboyant, generous, brave.

MOTHER MADELEINE—Humorous, somewhat frazzled, a member of the French resistance.

MAN WITH THE FLOWER IN HIS LAPEL—English, clipped, a very capable undercover agent.

SYNOPSIS OF SCENES AND MUSICAL NUMBERS
The action takes place from June 13th to June 18th, 1940,
between Paris and the Atlantic Coast of France.

ACT ONE

Prologue
    "I'LL BE HERE TOMORROW" .... *Jacobowsky*
Scene 1: Square Outside the Hotel de La Rose
    "FOR POLAND" ... *The Colonel, Mme. Bouffier and Parisians*
Scene 2: Saint-Cyrille
    "I BELONG HERE" .... *Marianne*
    "MARIANNE" .... *The Colonel*
Scene 3: A Local Train Heading West
    "WE'RE ALMOST THERE" .... *Marianne, Szabuniewicz,*
Jacobowsky, The Colonel,
Elegant Woman, Conductor and Passengers
Scene 4: Wagons of the Carnival Manzoni
    "MARIANNE" Reprise .... *Jacobowsky*
Scene 5: Open Spot in Countryside Near Rennes
    "MORE AND MORE/LESS AND LESS" .... *Marianne*
and the Colonel
Scene 6: Dressing Area of the Carnival Manzoni
    "ONE EXTRAORDINARY THING" .... *Jacobowsky,*
Marianne, The Colonel,
Szabuniewicz and the Carnival Manzoni
Scene 7: Midway of the Carnival Manzoni
    "ONE EXTRAORDINARY THING" Reprise ..... *Jacobowsky*

ACT TWO

Scene 1: A Tree-lined Canal in the West of France
    "MRS. S. L. JACOBOWSKY" .... *Jacobowsky*
Scene 2: Cafe of Papa Clairon at St. Nazaire
    "WEDDING CONVERSATION" .... *Jacobowsky*
and Bride's Father
    "MAZELTOV" .... *Bride's Father and Wedding Guests*
Scene 3: A Country Road Near St. Nazaire
    "I THINK, I THINK" .... *The Colonel*
Scene 4: 23 Rue Mace
    "FOR POLAND" Reprise .... *Marianne, Mother Madeleine*
and Sisters of Charity

6

The Grand Tour

PROLOGUE

At end of OVERTURE the CURTAIN rises on a MAN standing in silhouette on the bare stage. He wears a shiny but neat suit, bowler hat, carries several well-worn suitcases. As LIGHTS come up he steps forward, removes his hat, and says . . .

JACOBOWSKY. Flight is such a desperate word, I prefer migrations. It has a more optimistic definition; "To remove one's residence from one place to another." For birds that means to fly away to a warmer climate. Substitute "to stay alive" for "warmer climate" and you have my case precisely. (*With a bow.*) Jacobowsky. S. L. Jacobowsky. At present a Frenchman but I don't imagine that happy state will continue indefinitely. But I'm used to it, I've spent all my life in a futile attempt to become the citizen of some country. Any country. Do you know I speak seven languages fluently? Wrongly, but fluently. In the technique of flight Jacobowsky is unfortunately a virtuoso. Yes, I suppose it *is* flight when you come right down to it. But migration has a more hopeful sound. (*As MUSIC comes up.*) Migration number one! Poland to Germany. (*And he sings.*)
MAMA TOOK THE DISHES
THE FURNITURE
MAMA TOOK THE PILLOWS
THE CANDLESTICKS
MAMA TOOK THE CHILDREN
AND FLED TO BERLIN . . .
I GREW INTO MANHOOD
A CITIZEN
I WENT INTO BUSINESS
A PATRIOT
FOOLISHLY BELIEVING
I BELONGED IN BERLIN . . .
. . . My incurable optimism!
THEN THAT KNOCK ON THE DOOR
IN THE DEAD OF THE NIGHT
AND THAT VOICE SAYING
RUN, THE SKY IS FALLING

RUN, THE SHIP IS SINKING
THROUGH THE BLIND CONFUSION
I REMEMBER STILL WHAT I WAS THINKING . . .
I'LL BE HERE TOMORROW
ALIVE AND WELL AND THRIVING
I'LL BE HERE TOMORROW
MY TALENT IS SURVIVING
IF BEFORE THE DAWN THIS FRAGILE WORLD MIGHT
    CRACK
SOMEONE'S GOTTA TRY TO PUT THE PIECES BACK
SO, FROM BENEATH THE RUBBLE
YOU'LL HEAR A LITTLE VOICE
SAY "LIFE IS WORTH THE TROUBLE"
HAVE YOU A BETTER CHOICE?
SO LET THE SKEPTICS SAY "TONIGHT WE'RE DEAD
    AND GONE"
I'LL BE HERE TOMORROW
SIMPLY GOING ON!
    (JACOBOWSKY *confidently soars into his dance step, then it peters
    off as he says.*)
    . . . Migration Number Two! Berlin to Vienna.
    (*And he sings.*)
WE MOVED TO VIENNA, THE CITY OF WALTZES
OF STRUDEL AND GLITTER AND GOLD
WE MOVED TO VIENNA, BUT UNDER THE WALTZES
A STRANGE COUNTER MELODY
RUTHLESS AND COLD—
RUN, YOUR LIFE'S IN DANGER
RUN, YOU'VE BEEN DEFEATED
RACING THROUGH THE NIGHT
I LOOKED UP AT THE STARS AS I REPEATED . . .

I'LL BE HERE TOMORROW
ALIVE AND WELL AND THRIVING
I'LL BE HERE TOMORROW
MY TALENT IS SURVIVING
IF BEFORE THE DAWN THIS FRAGILE WORLD MIGHT
    CRACK
SOMEONE'S GOTTA TRY TO PUT THE PIECES BACK
SO, FROM BENEATH THE RUBBLE
YOU'LL HEAR A LITTLE VOICE
SAY "LIFE IS WORTH THE TROUBLE"

HAVE YOU A BETTER CHOICE?
SO LET THE SKEPTICS SAY "TONIGHT WE'RE DEAD
        AND GONE"
I'LL BE HERE TOMORROW
SIMPLY GOING ON!

TO PARIS
TO PARIS
THE CITY OF FREEDOM AND WONDER AND MUSIC
        AND LIGHT
BUT EVEN
IN PARIS
I'M DREADING THAT KNOCK ON THE DOOR
IN THE DEAD OF THE NIGHT—
RUN, THE SKY IS FALLING
RUN, THE SHIP IS SINKING
WHEN THAT MOMENT HAPPENS
YOU KNOW VERY WELL WHAT I'LL BE
        THINKING . . .
    (*The orchestra plays the melody of the chorus as* JACOBOWSKY
    *takes a deep breath, clenches his fists with new determination,
    then sings.*)
SOMEONE'S GOTTA TRY TO PUT THE PIECES BACK
SO, FROM BENEATH THE RUBBLE
YOU'LL HEAR A LITTLE VOICE
SAY "LIFE IS WORTH THE TROUBLE"
HAVE YOU A BETTER CHOICE
SO LET THE SKEPTICS SAY "TONIGHT WE'RE DEAD
        AND GONE"
I'LL BE HERE TOMORROW
SIMPLY GOING ON!

(*Through last of this a STREET IN PARIS has come on and now, as
        SONG ends, we hear air raid siren wailing as* VARIOUS PEOPLE
        scurry for shelter and we find ourselves   . . .)

ACT ONE

SCENE 1

In front of the HOTEL MON REPOS ET DE LA ROSE, a fourth-class establishment somewhere in Montmartre. A YOUNG MAN WEARING APRON *takes* JACOBOWSKY'S *suitcases and brings them inside hotel as* JACOBOWSKY *looks at his watch and crosses to small cafe table Left. Through this we become aware of aristocratic-looking* MAN IN OFFICER'S UNIFORM *who sits unconcernedly eating breakfast at table Right as last of* PARISIANS *scurry off. A very nervous* MAN WITH PINCE-NEZ *stands alongside him.*

MAN WITH PINCE-NEZ. . . . Colonel Stjerbinsky, I presume you heard the air raid alert! Wouldn't it be wiser to continue our discussion inside.

COLONEL. If and when we see the planes there will be enough time to take shelter, now what is it you interrupt my breakfast with?

MAN WITH PINCE-NEZ. Only the documents you are supposed to be waiting for, or have you forgotten why you are here?

COLONEL. I forget nothing! (*At the top of his voice as* MAN WITH PINCE-NEZ *tries to quiet him.*) . . . Polish government in exile assigns me to bring addresses of our resistance fighters in occupied Poland to London so that struggle for freedom for our valiant country can go on! Give.

MAN WITH PINCE-NEZ. (*Handing him papers.*) Everything is in this envelope. You will proceed from here to St. Nazaire where you will meet a man with a flower in his buttonhole in the cafe of Papa Clairon. He will offer you a drink, you will give the signal To Liberty!, and he will arrange passage on the boat to England. And I must impress on you that the boat leaves on Saturday, six days from today, and if you are not there it sails without you!

COLONEL. (*Backing him angrily off Left as* SZABUNIEWICZ, *the* COLONEL'S *orderly, starts out of hotel.*) And I must impress on you, my desk bureaucrat, that I have fought the Nazis on the Vistula and the Somme and to aid my beloved country, I swim to London if necessary! (*But he is gone. To* SZABUNIEWICZ.) . . . Szabuniewicz, we leave Paris this afternoon. Get me place on plane.

SZABUNIEWICZ. But last plane leaved yesterday.

COLONEL. Then we go by car!

SZABUNIEWICZ. Vice-council go off Tuesday, he take all four cars.

COLONEL. Then call somebody, get me horse, mule, anything!

JACOBOWSKY. (*As* SZABUNIEWICZ *hurries into hotel and* MME. BOUFFIER, *the proprietor, starts out and begins hastily clearing table.*) . . . Colonel, my name is Jacobowsky, in a certain sense a countryman, I too was born in Poland.

COLONEL. (*Turning away after a sharp glance.*) About that there is nothing I can do.

JACOBOWSKY. I overheard you discussing a means of locomotion to leave Paris and as I too am in the same position, I thought we might leave the city together.

COLONEL. When I travel with company, it is company *I* choose. Now if you will excuse me, Monsieur Liebowitz . . .

JACOBOWSKY. Yes, Jacobowsky, you see I have a rendezvous with a gentleman who might have a car for sale so it occurred to me that we . . .

COLONEL. Again the we! Monsieur Wohlfson, let me make one thing clear. There is no we, no us, no two, no both, just me. Good day.

MME. BOUFFIER. (*Anxiously, as* COLONEL *exits into hotel.*) . . . Dear Monsieur Jacobowsky, you must come inside! Didn't you hear the sirens? Your gentleman with the car is hardly coming in the middle of an alert . . . (*There is sound of an imposing car horn off Left.*) There is a divine providence! Monsieur Jacobowsky, it's a Rolls Royce.

JACOBOWSKY. How divine of providence to provide so divinely.

(*MUSIC up as* MME. BOUFFIER *hurries into hotel and elegant chauffeur-driven open touring car comes on.*)

CHAUFFEUR. (*As he stops car, alights.*) Well, Monsieur, here it is! The last car for sale in the entire city of Paris and it will cost you a mere fleabite. Forty thousand francs.

JACOBOWSKY. Your flea bites off an arm and a leg, thank you very much for your trouble, goodbye.

CHAUFFEUR. (*As* JACOBOWSKY *starts to hotel.*) Did I say forty, I meant thirty!

JACOBOWSKY. Monsieur, I should like nothing more than to spend a pleasant morning negotiating with you but I think it better to face facts. The Germans will be here any minute, fact? Fact. They will requisition this car, fact? Fact. You must either sell it now or dump it in the river, fact? Fact. (*Taking out money, counting bills.*) . . . Now at five thousand a fact, that's fifteen thousand francs.

CHAUFFEUR. Fifteen thousand? Monsieur, for the sake of my children . . .

JACOBOWSKY. For the sake of your children, sixteen thousand.

CHAUFFEUR. You are taking advantage of a soldier of Verdun!

JACOBOWSKY. For the sake of Verdun, seventeen thousand.

CHAUFFEUR. Wait, I have another point . . .

JACOBOWSKY. For the sake of not finding it, eighteen thousand, but that is all!

CHAUFFEUR. Done! (*Taking bills.*) . . . I do not wish to make you unhappy, Monsieur, but I would have taken twelve.

JACOBOWSKY. I do not wish to ruin your day, Monsieur, but I would have paid fifty. (CHAUFFEUR *hands him key.*) . . . What is that?

CHAUFFEUR. (*As he exits.*) The ignition key.

JACOBOWSKY. The ignition key, what's an ignition key? Oh my God, it just occurs to me that I don't know how to drive! (*To* YOUNG MAN WEARING APRON *who comes out of hotel with his suitcases.*) . . . Jeannot, do you know anything about cars?

JEANNOT. No, Monsieur, only bicycles. Where shall I put the suitcases?

JACOBOWSKY. In the back seat but what's the use, if the car won't move neither will they. (*To* MME. BOUFFIER *who appears with remainder of his things.*) . . . Madame Bouffier, do you know how to operate this machine?

MME. BOUFFIER. No, Monsieur. A sewing machine, yes. Is it the same principle?

JACOBOWSKY. I see no place for the thread. (*As he twists wheel, pulls gears.*) . . . There must be a way, there is always a way, it's just a question of finding it . . . (*Through this the* COLONEL *starts out followed by* SZABUNIEWICZ *laden with trunks, etc.*)

COLONEL. What do you mean you have not found transportation? I ordered you to find transportation and will not accept anything but success!

SZABUNIEWICZ. But is no transportation left in city; not car, not horse, not carriage, not mule, not nothing. (*He sees car.*) . . . Oh my God.

JACOBOWSKY. (*Honking horn.*) Colonel, are you by any chance an automobilist?

COLONEL. Szabuniewicz, I do not know why it concerns this man but for sake of explanation you may tell him I am cavalryist.

JACOBOWSKY. But modern cavalry is usually motorized.

COLONEL. (*With simple pride.*) Not in Poland.

JACOBOWSKY. Colonel, does this mean you can drive or not?

COLONEL. If road is straight I can drive, curves I do not care to see. (*As he starts Left.*) . . . Come Szabuniewicz, we start walking!

JACOBOWSKY. Excuse me, Colonel, but the Germans, as you know, are on the outskirts of Paris.

COLONEL. Aha, you are afraid for your skin!

JACOBOWSKY. Yes, Colonel. My skin and the skin of those fighters for Polish freedom on that list you are taking to England.

COLONEL. What? You interested in Polish freedom too?

JACOBOWSKY. It is the first of my native lands. I was born in Studno near Kasimisz.

COLONEL. Studno near Kasimisz! My father owned great estates in Kasimisz. And your father?

JACOBOWSKY. A scholar. He taught biblical history to children.

SZABUNIEWICZ. (*Trying to encourage the* COLONEL *to accept* JACOBOWSKY *and his car.*) Good profession! (*After a look from the* COLONEL.) . . . Of course their bible incorrect.

JACOBOWSKY. Precisely why it might be interesting to travel together, you could point out where Moses went wrong.

COLONEL. (*Shaking his head.*) No, is against every principle of Stjerbinsky code to accommodate a creature such as this! (*And he sings.*)

MY CODE OF HONOR SAYS "MEN ARE BROTHERS"
THAT I SHOULD SPREAD MY ARMS AND HUG THE
    WORLD EN MASSE
LOVE GOD ALMIGHTY ABOVE ALL OTHERS
WHO HAD THE WISDOM TO HAVE MADE ME UPPER
    CLASS
THAT I'M A MAN WHO LOVES HIS NEIGHBORS IS AN
    UNDISPUTED FACT
BUT YOU, MY FRIEND, MAKE PREJUDICE AN
    HONORABLE ACT!
AS I'M WHO I AM, YOU ARE WHO YOU ARE
AND SO MONSIEUR, I WILL NOT DRIVE THIS CAR!

JACOBOWSKY.

AT LEAST, DO IT FOR POLAND
FOR A MEAL OF PEROGI AND BIGOS
AND BABKA AND TEA
AND THIS PLEASANT LITTLE RIDE
CAN BRING YOU PATRIOTIC PRIDE

IF YOU DO IT FOR P-O-L-A-N-D
COME ON, DO IT FOR POLAND
FOR KEEPING THE FATHERLAND OUT AND THE
    MOTHERLAND FREE
THOUGH YOUR ATTITUDE IS STOIC
THEY'LL CONSIDER YOU HEROIC
IF YOU DO IT FOR P-O-L-A-N-D!

COLONEL. (*Looking at* JACOBOWSKY, *then shaking his head as he moves away.*)

THOUGH LIFE IS BUILT ON COMPROMISE I KNOW
I NEVER THOUGHT I'D HAVE TO STOOP THIS LOW

JACOBOWSKY.

AT LEAST, DO IT FOR POLAND
SO THE SAUSAGE'LL KEEP GETTING STUFFED AND
    THE SHEEP'LL GET SHORN
AND YOU'LL SOON EXCHANGE YOUR PALLOR
FOR THE ROSY GLOW OF VALOR
WHEN YOU DO IT FOR THE LAND WHERE YOU WERE
    BORN
COME ON, DO IT FOR POLAND
PADEREWSKI, PILSUDSKI, AND CHOPIN WOULD
    SURELY AGREE
THAT THIS DEED THAT YOU ARE DOUBTING
WILL BECOME A SUMMER OUTING
WHEN YOU DO IT FOR P-O-L-A-N-D
FOR THE FOLKS IN GDYNIA
IT'S A PEACH OF A TOWN
FOR THE MEN IN THE SALT MINES

(*Waving a small Polish flag he takes out of his briefcase.*)

WE CAN'T LET THEM DOWN!

COLONEL. (*Unable to resist any longer.*)

ALL RIGHT, I'LL DO IT FOR POLAND!
FOR KEEPING THE FATHERLAND OUT AND THE
    MOTHERLAND FREE
THIS HORRENDOUS TRIP I'M TAKING
AND THE SACRIFICE I'M MAKING
I'LL BE MAKING FOR P-O-L-A-N-D . . .

(*As MUSIC continues.*)

. . . Now, my first order is to clear this trash out of back seat.

JACOBOWSKY. (*As* SZABUNIEWICZ *begins removing his possessions.*) Excuse me, Colonel, but those rugs belonged to my mother and they mean very much to me.

COLONEL. I am one of Pilsudski's Colonels, Liebowitz, and not used to voyaging in furniture truck! (*As he gets out of car and* JACOBOWSKY *rallies* MME. BOUFFIER *and* ALL NEIGHBORS *to help him.*) . . . Is no use. I should have known better than to listen to such a creature in the first place. Now take my trunk and we start walking. In one day strong man can cover fifty kilometers . . .

MME. BOUFFIER/OTHERS. (*Interrupting* COLONEL *as they sing.*)
AT LEAST, DO IT FOR POLAND
PADEREWSKI, PILSUDSKI, AND CHOPIN WOULD
    SURELY AGREE
THAT YOU'LL SOON EXCHANGE YOUR PALLOR
FOR THE ROSY GLOW OF VALOR
WHEN YOU DO IT FOR P-O-L-A-N-D!
   (*SONG becomes staged movement as French tricolor banner is brought on,* JACOBOWSKY *pins up the blue stripe to make it into the red and white flag of Poland, they finally surround the* COLONEL *with the flag as they sing.*)
COME ON, DO IT FOR POLAND
FOR KEEPING THE FATHERLAND OUT AND THE
    MOTHERLAND FREE
AND THIS PLEASANT LITTLE RIDE
CAN BRING YOU PATRIOTIC PRIDE
IF YOU DO IT FOR P-O-L-A-N-D . . .
   (*Variously.*)
FOR GENERAL PULASKI!
FOR MADAME CURIE!
FOR KELBASI SAUSAGE!
   JACOBOWSKY.
FOR STUDNO NEAR KASIMISZ!
   ALL. (*As* COLONEL *gives in, they lead him to car, he gets into driver's seat as* SZABUNIEWICZ *and* JACOBOWSKY *climb aboard.*)
I'LL (YOU'LL) BE MAKING FOR P-O-L-A-N-D!

JACOBOWSKY. (*Taking out map as* STREET IN PARIS *starts off one side, car starts off the other.*) . . . Our route is simple, Colonel. Down the main boulevard to Place de la Bastille, then west-southwest.

COLONEL. You are wrong, Yalofsky. West-*north*west.

JACOBOWSKY. But west-northwest is where the Germans are.

COLONEL. I cannot help it if they also choose my route. I have an appointment with a lady in St. Cyrille, and that is the direction I am going. (*By now they are out in countryside as* COLONEL *continues.*) . . . But do not despair, Yacowitz! I have outwitted the Nazis before and I will again.

JACOBOWSKY. I am a long way from despair, Colonel. My poor

mother, wise woman that she was, always used to say that no matter how hopeless things appeared, there are always two possibilities. Even now, either I succeed in escaping from the German or I don't succeed. If I succeed that's good, but if I don't succeed there are still two possibilities. Either they put me in a good concentration camp or a bad concentration camp. If it's a good concentration camp that's not exactly good but it's bearable . . . but if it's a bad concentration camp there are still two possibilities . . . (*By now car is off and we are up on* . . .

ACT ONE

SCENE 2

A squad of GERMAN SOLDIERS *advancing through the French countryside. Sporadic machine-gun fire, the* GERMANS *exit Right, and we find ourselves in front of a GARDEN WALL IN ST. CYRILLE early that evening. An* OLD WOMAN *marches determinedly on carrying several suitcases and a birdcage. She sets them down as* MARIANNE, *a lovely and vivacious young Frenchwoman, appears behind her.*

MARIANNE. . . . Madame Vauclain, what are you doing?

MME. VAUCLAIN. Getting your things ready. The Germans will be here any minute, you must leave at once.

MARIANNE. I will do nothing of the kind! This is my home and no Germans are going to make me leave it! And what would the children say if their teacher ran away?

MME. VAUCLAIN. That you were being sensible. And you needn't worry about your precious house, in twenty-four hours everything in St. Cyrille will belong to the Germans anyhow.

MARIANNE. I'm not so sure about that. The man I love, Colonel Tadeusz Boleslav Stjerbinsky, has sworn to return with men and planes and crush the Boches forever!

MME. VAUCLAIN. He will not return! France is defeated! Will you give up your freedom for a few meters of rocks and dirt?

MARIANNE. These few meters of rocks and dirt as you call them are my home. I was born in this house, so was my father and his father and no Germans are going to make me leave it.

(*MUSIC comes up and she sings.*)

I BELONG HERE

WHERE A DUSTY ROAD CURLS BY
YES, I BELONG HERE
WHERE THE BIRCHES TOUCH THE SKY
THERE'S NOTHING SPLENDID
OR REMARKABLE IN ANY WAY
BUT I OPEN THE SHUTTER EACH DAY
AND IT DAZZLES MY EYE . . .
THERE'S A SCHOOLHOUSE
AND A NOISY COUNTRY STORE
A HILL OF LILAC
AND A BRIDGE AND NOT MUCH MORE
AND SO IF ONE DAY
TO THE ENDS OF THE EARTH I MAY ROAM—
I'LL STILL BELONG HERE
I'LL BELONG HERE
ON THIS SPECK OF EARTH I CALL HOME!
    (*We hear the sound of an airplane overhead.* MARIANNE *looks up
    as MUSIC continues.*)
    . . . The bedroom windows, I haven't drawn the blackout curtains!
(*Taking suitcase before* MME. VAUCLAIN *can protest.*) Now I don't
want to hear another word about it, just take in the rest of those
suitcases. (*As* MME. VAUCLAIN *gathers cases.*) . . . And don't
forget Lulu! (MME. VAUCLAIN *picks up birdcage, goes muttering
back into house, as* MARIANNE *continues.*)
SO IF ONE DAY
TO THE ENDS OF THE EARTH
I MAY ROAM
I'LL STILL BELONG HERE
I'LL BELONG HERE
ON THIS SPECK OF EARTH
I CALL HOME.

(*She exits, and the garden is silent. A moment, then in the distance
    we hear the sound of an exhausted motor coughing and sputter-
    ing. We reprise MUSIC of "FOR POLAND" as sound grows
    louder and louder and* JACOBOWSKY'S *limousine starts jerkily
    on from Right. Steam is hissing out of radiator, one tire is flat,
    the car is covered with mud and dust. It gives one final gasp
    then shudders to a stop.*)

COLONEL. At last we arrive at the object of my heart's desire!
JACOBOWSKY. Also one half day closer to the Germans. Colonel,
you will never know what these twelve hours have cost me.

COLONEL. Polish government in exile will pay you back your cost! Szabuniewicz, child, write down everything we owe this merchant.

SZABUNIEWICZ. Have no paper, in head is written.

JACOBOWSKY. Good, then in your head write that the Polish government owes me the following: Replacement One, a heart which has begun to flutter like a wounded bird; Replacement Two, one wrecked nervous system. And if the Germans catch me, one entire Jacobowsky. Colonel, I don't understand you. You seem to look down on the human instinct of self-preservation.

COLONEL. In your case this ambition is trivial. (*He looks to* SZABUNIEWICZ *and they both laugh.*) . . . Szabuniewicz, my comb. And the looking glass.

JACOBOWSKY. (*Throwing up his hands as* SZABUNIEWICZ *gets toilet kit from car.*) Reason rebels! Colonel, there is no doubt that you have one of the finest minds of the fifteenth century; unfortunately I live in the twentieth.

COLONEL. I hate twentieth century! No style, no elegance, everything in this damn century got to make sense! Where is poetry, where is heroism!

JACOBOWSKY. Colonel, I implore you, be heroic, rescue your lady and let's go!

SZABUNIEWICZ. Windows is dark, maybe lady is sleeping. I blow horn to wake her.

COLONEL. You wake lady with automobile horn, I break your hands! Music, Szabuniewicz! We wake her sweet.

JACOBOWSKY. (*As* SZABUNIEWICZ *takes out his mouth organ, begins softly playing.*) I am imagining things! The entire German army within shouting distance and he picks this moment to give a recital. (*As he takes jerrycan from car, starts off.*) . . . Did I say fifteenth century? Twelfth. (*As he exits.*) B.C.

(*The* COLONEL *now positions himself just outside the garden wall as he sings.*)

COLONEL.
DON'T EVER TELL ME THAT YOU'VE HEARD THE
    CELLO
FOR YOU'VE NEVER MET MARIANNE
DON'T TALK OF SILVER OR VIOLET OR YELLOW
FOR YOU'VE NEVER MET MARIANNE
DON'T MENTION GARNETS OR PEARLS FROM MANILA

FORGET THEM AS FAST AS YOU CAN
DON'T SPEAK OF GINGER OR LIME OR VANILLA
UNTIL YOU HAVE KISSED MARIANNE

DON'T EVER MENTION THE LIGHTS FROM THE
     PLANETS
FOR YOU'VE NEVER SEEN MARIANNE
YOU'LL PITY THE JENNIES, THE JANES, AND THE
     JANETS
THE MOMENT YOU'VE SEEN MARIANNE
AND SO THE ONE THING I'M POSITIVE OF IS
THAT GOD MADE ME ONE LUCKY MAN
GENTLEMEN, SORRY . . . YOU WON'T KNOW WHAT
     LOVE IS
UNTIL YOU HAVE LOVED MARIANNE!

(*At end of first chorus, a light comes up in window and* MARIANNE
     hurries out.)

    MARIANNE. (*As MUSIC continues.*) Tadeusz!
    COLONEL. I have return!
    MARIANNE. I knew you would!
    COLONEL. Come, my arms wait to receive you! (*She runs to his
arms, he holds her and sings.*)
AND SO THE ONE THING I'M POSITIVE OF IS
THAT GOD MADE ME ONE LUCKY MAN
GENTLEMEN, SORRY . . . YOU WON'T KNOW WHAT
     LOVE IS
UNTIL YOU HAVE LOVED MARIANNE!
    (*As SONG ends and he releases* MARIANNE.)
. . . And now, my life, please pack your things. We go to England
to join Polish government in exile.
    MARIANNE. But the men, the planes . . .
    COLONEL. Did not materialize, so we go.
    MARIANNE. No, Tadeusz, I would do anything in this world for
you but that. I will never leave my land.
    COLONEL. I leave my land. Szabuniewicz leave his. (JACOB-
OWSKY *has returned through last of this, now taps* COLONEL *on
shoulder.*)
    JACOBOWSKY. Begging your pardon, Colonel . . .
    COLONEL. Not now.
    JACOBOWSKY. I could not help overhearing your conversation

COLONEL. I said not now!

MARIANNE. Tadeusz, who is this man?

COLONEL. One S. L. Jacobowsky, not important . . .

JACOBOWSKY. The Colonel is right, Mademoiselle, I am not important but what I have to say might be. There are times when in order to advance one must retreat; this is one of those times.

MARIANNE. What do you mean?

JACOBOWSKY. You may have to fight to win back your home and you cannot fight unless you are free. Remain here and by tomorrow morning you will no longer be free.

COLONEL. I do not need you to speak for me, Monsieur!

JACOBOWSKY. (*Briskly.*) It will save time; you have the same thoughts as I do but it sometimes takes you too long to gather them. To come back here, Mademoiselle, he risked his life!

MARIANNE. Tadeusz . . .

JACOBOWSKY. What's more, he risked mine. Did he do that for nothing? Abandon your home, Mademoiselle, in order to save your home!

MARIANNE. (*To* COLONEL.) Your friend is persuasive.

COLONEL. Is not friend, merely travelling acquaintance.

MARIANNE. But amusing and sympathetic. (*Making up her mind.*) . . . Very well, I'll go. Give me two minutes to bring my things out to the car.

JACOBOWSKY. Alas, Mademoiselle, we're out of gas and there's none to be had in St. Cyrille, but I did take the liberty of looking up the railway schedules and there's a local train due any minute for Evron. Shall I give you a hand?

COLONEL. Stay where you are! Szabuniewicz, you will help Mademoiselle Marianne with her things.

JACOBOWSKY. (*As* SZABUNIEWICZ *and* MARIANNE *start into the house.*) . . . You are very fortunate, Colonel. She's a lovely young woman.

COLONEL. Is not for you to notice if she lovely or not!

JACOBOWSKY. Only a dead man could avoid noticing.

COLONEL. (*Menacingly.*) That can be arranged. (SZABUNIEWICZ *has appeared with two heavy suitcases.*) . . . Szabuniewicz, what is this?

SZABUNIEWICZ. (*As* MARIANNE *follows with hatbox, birdcage.*) Is belongings of Mademoiselle Marianne.

COLONEL. But there will be no room!

JACOBOWSKY. Room is elastic, it can be made to expand. (*As he takes suitcases.*) . . . Colonel, you are a great man but as a refugee

I am more experienced and nothing is so warming in difficult hours than to have a few familiar knickknacks with you. It gives you a link with the past, a bridge to what you were.

MARIANNE. You are so understanding, Monsieur Jacobowsky.

COLONEL. (*At the top of his voice.*) All right, take whole damn business! You see, I am understanding too.

MARIANNE. (*As she takes hat out of box.*) I suppose I could leave the hatbox . . .

SZABUNIEWICZ. Colonel . . .

COLONEL. Not now.

SZABUNIEWICZ. Colonel, sew papers in lady's hat.

COLONEL. What you say?

SZABUNIEWICZ. Hide Polish government papers in lady's hat.

COLONEL. (*Repeating.*) Hide papers in hat . . . (*Then as if it were his idea.*) Attention! I have important idea! We *take* hatbox! And in your hat, Marianne, we sew documents for Polish government in exile! Germans will never look for them there.

JACOBOWSKY. Colonel, it's an inspiration!

MARIANNE. And it will make me feel so important! I'll do it right this minute.

MME. VAUCLAIN. (*Hurrying out of house through above.*) Mademoiselle Marianne, if you are leaving you must go now! It's on the radio, the Nazis are in Rocheville, that's only ten kilometers away!

COLONEL. Very well, we load everything in car and drive to station.

JACOBOWSKY. (*As* SZABUNIEWICZ *begins loading car.*) But there's no gas, Colonel, the car won't move!

COLONEL. (*As he helps* MARIANNE *into car.*) There are other means of locomotion besides gasoline, Jacobowsky.

JACOBOWSKY. (*Rolling up sleeves, going to back of car.*) Say no more, my people are used to it, look at the pyramids, release the brake, Colonel, it'll help . . . (*As MUSIC comes up and he and* SZABUNIEWICZ *begins pushing car.*) Now sit back, relax, and enjoy the scenery.

MARIANNE. Monsieur Jacobowsky, you sound just like a guide!

JACOBOWSKY. (*As they exit.*) Think of me as that, dear lady! And now if you'll all make yourselves comfortable, the Grand Tour begins!

(*By now they are off as TRAIN starts on and we are up on* . . .

ACT ONE

Scene 3

THIRD CLASS CARRIAGE OF LOCAL TRAIN as Conductor, Various Passengers, *start on.*

Conductor. . . . All aboard, seven-oh-three to Evron, into the carriage please, all aboard!

Jacobowsky. (*Coming on with luggage followed by* Szabuniewicz, Marianne *and the* Colonel.) Right this way, Colonel! The train is waiting.

Colonel. Stop, Szabuniewicz! Do not put my luggage aboard. This carriage not first class.

Jacobowsky. May I point out, Colonel, that what makes a carriage first class is not the number painted on the door but the quality of the passengers inside.

Szabuniewicz. (*Seeing where* Jacobowsky *is heading.*) Because Colonel is first class, car becomes first class!

Marianne. Exactly! If we treat this car as a first-class Pullman, that's what it becomes. (*And she sings.*)
THIS OLD TRAIN
IS POOR AND TIRED
SO YOUR COOPERATION IS URGENTLY REQUIRED
ALTHOUGH WE'RE ALL EMBARKING ON A LONG AND
    DISMAL TRIP
IT'S NOT TOO BAD IF YOU JUST ADD SOME FRENCH
    STIFF UPPER LIP
    (*Train has begun slowly moving now and* Various Other Passengers, *loaded down with luggage, run to leap aboard and crowd into compartment as she continues.*)
WE'RE ALMOST THERE
WE'RE ALMOST THERE
THOUGH THERE'S A MILLION MORE KILOMETERS TO
    GO
THE WINDOW CLATTERS
THE ENGINE SPATTERS
BUT WITH A GLASS OF WINE, YOU'LL NEVER KNOW
A SPICY JOKE
A HAND OF BRIDGE
AND WE'LL FORGET THE TRIP IS TEDIOUS AND SLOW
THE CAR IS MUSTY
THE TRACK IS RUSTY

WE'LL END UP GOD KNOWS WHERE
BUT WITH DIVERSION
IT'S AN EXCURSION!
AND SO WE'RE ALMOST THERE!

(*The* COLONEL *is now wedged in between a crate of chickens and a*
    LARGE MAN *eating a pungent sausage as* SZABUNIEWICZ *joins*
    MARIANNE.)

MARIANNE/SZABUNIEWICZ.
A LITTLE STROLL
FROM CAR TO CAR
TO FEEL THE SPIRIT OF THE CROWD BEGIN TO
    GROW
SZABUNIEWICZ.
THE ROOF IS LEAKING
MARIANNE.
THE WHEELS ARE SHRIEKING
MARIANNE/SZABUNIEWICZ.
BUT WE SAY C'EST LA GUERRE
THERE'S HELL BEFORE US
BUT ONE MORE CHORUS
AND LOOK—WE'RE ALMOST THERE!

(*The* OTHER PASSENGERS *have watched this futile attempt to cheer
    the* COLONEL, *now try their hand as they sing.*)

CONDUCTOR.
WE'RE ALMOST THERE
ONE PASSENGER.
WE'RE ALMOST THERE
SEVERAL PASSENGERS.
WE MUST ARRIVE BEFORE THE ROQUEFORT GETS
    TOO STRONG
TWO WOMEN.
SOME CONVERSATION
TWO MEN.
SOME RECREATION
JACOBOWSKY.
PERHAPS MADAME MIGHT OFFER US A SONG
VARIOUS GROUPS. (*As* ELEGANT LADY *sings obligatti.*)
A LITTLE BREAD
A LITTLE BRIE

TO HELP FORGET THE TRIP'S TOO LUMPY AND TOO
    LONG
    ALL PASSENGERS.
THE MOTOR GRUMBLES
A CANNON RUMBLES
AND GIVES US QUITE A SCARE
    CONDUCTOR.
IT'S ROUGH AND RISKY
    ONE PASSENGER.
BUT HAVE A WHISKEY
    ALL.
AND LOOK—WE'RE ALMOST THERE!
    JACOBOWSKY. (*Taking* CONDUCTOR'S *hat and becoming Tour
Guide as* OTHER PASSENGERS *laugh at his jokes to try to encourage
the glum-looking* COLONEL *to do the same.*)
THIS OLD TRAIN
IS POOR AND TIRED
SO YOUR IMAGINATION IS URGENTLY REQUIRED
SEE THAT QUAINT OLD FACTORY IN YONDER GLADE
THAT'S THE PLACE WHERE LOUIS FIFTEENTH CHAIRS
    ARE MADE.
    (COLONEL *doesn't react.*)
AND ON THE LEFT
THAT GREAT BIG BLUR
I PROMISE YOU THAT THAT'S THE BACK OF THE
    SACRE COEUR
THAT POPLAR PLAYED A NOBLE ROLE IN HISTORY
NAPOLEON RELIEVED HIMSELF BEHIND THAT TREE
    (*Still nothing.*)
THAT CURL OF SMOKE
THAT STAINS THE SKY
WOULD YOU BELIEVE THAT COMES FROM A
    CHIMNEY AT VERSAILLES?
AND SEE THAT LOVELY HORSE THAT'S GRAZING
    THERE AT THE GATE
THE GRANDPA OF THAT HORSE MADE LOVE TO
    CATHERINE THE GREAT
I TELL YOU
THIS OLD TRAIN
IS QUITE A MESS
BUT IF YOU CLOSE YOUR EYES YOU'RE ON THE
    ORIENT EXPRESS

ALL. (*The mood becoming quite festive as* COLONEL *sinks lower and lower in his seat.*)
A LITTLE BREAD
A LITTLE BRIE
TO HELP FORGET THE TRIP'S TOO LUMPY AND TOO
     LONG
THE MOTOR GRUMBLES
A CANNON RUMBLES
AND GIVES US QUITE A SCARE
IT'S ROUGH AND RISKY
BUT HAVE A WHISKEY
AND LOOK—WE'RE ALMOST THERE!
(*The festivities grow as food and wine are passed around, cards are dealt, jokes are told, bottoms are pinched,* PEASANT LADY *gets up and throws her scarf around waist of* JACOBOWSKY *and they begin to DANCE. Suddenly* SZABUNIEWICZ, *who has gotten carried away with the festivities, falls off platform at end of carriage. As* VARIOUS PASSENGERS *desperately lean out doors and windows to try to haul him back aboard, he slips further and further behind.* JACOBOWSKY *rushes to rear platform of train, leans out, and tries to grab his fingertips as SONG continues.*)
WE'RE ALMOST THERE
WE'RE ALMOST THERE
THOUGH THERE'S A MILLION MORE KILOMETERS TO
     GO
THE WINDOW CLATTERS
THE ENGINE SPATTERS
BUT WITH A GLASS OF WINE, YOU'LL NEVER KNOW
A SPICY JOKE
A HAND OF BRIDGE
AND WE'LL FORGET THE TRIP IS TEDIOUS AND SLOW
THE CAR IS MUSTY
THE TRACK IS RUSTY
WE'LL WIND UP GOD KNOWS WHERE
BUT WITH DIVERSION . . .
IT'S AN EXCURSION
AND SO WE'RE ALMOST, ALMOST THERE
(JACOBOWSKY *almost has him.*)
ALMOST, ALMOST THERE
(*He grabs his fingertips, and triumphantly hauls the exhausted* SZABUNIEWICZ *aboard as* EVERYBODY *sings.*)
WE'RE ALMOST THERE!

(*A shriek of brakes, the train lurches to a stop, and the NUMBER is over.*)

CONDUCTOR. (*Running along Downstage of train.*) . . . All off! Everybody must disembark! All off!

JACOBOWSKY. What is the problem, sir?

CONDUCTOR. The track up ahead is cut. The Germans, I expect. All off! Everybody must disembark!

JACOBOWSKY. Come along, Mademoiselle Marianne. (*To* SZABUNIEWICZ *as they start to push their way off train.*) . . . Szabuniewicz, get the Colonel!

COLONEL. Where we going? Do you expect to walk to St. Nazaire?

JACOBOWSKY. We passed some carnival wagons about a hundred meters back, perhaps we might persuade them to take us with them! You wait here. I'll be right back.

PASSENGERS. (*As* JACOBOWSKY *exits.*)
WE'RE ALMOST THERE
WE'RE ALMOST THERE
THOUGH THERE'S A MILLION MORE KILOMETERS TO
    GO,
THE TRACK IS RUSTY . . .

(*By now TRAIN has disappeared and we are up on* . . .

ACT ONE

SCENE 4

WAGONS OF THE CARNIVAL MANZONI, a rather dilapidated traveling circus. Motorized wooden caravans emblazoned with letters advertising "CARNIVAL MANZONI" and beneath that, "Featuring Hugo The Hungarian Hercules," accompanied by paintings of handsome man in tights doing sharp-shooting act, being shot out of cannon, etc. MUSICAL segue ends as last of PASSENGERS *disappear and* JACOBOWSKY *hurries back on with large sack.*

JACOBOWSKY. . . . A delightful surprise. The owner of the carnival is a most charming woman and she's agreed to take us all the way to St. Nazaire! Only one drawback, she's refused to take money so I made a little trade. You see the carnival needs a new barker's uniform so I . . . well, I . . . I . . .

COLONEL. (*Realizing.*) What? The uniform of one of Pilsudski's colonels you give to wear by barker in carnival? But this is garb of honor.

JACOBOWSKY. So now you will wear another uniform, the uniform of retreat.

MARIANNE. It's a blessing in disguise, Tadeusz. There are Germans everywhere. If they see you in that uniform, they'll arrest you.

COLONEL. Very well. This final humiliation I bear only for my beloved motherland! (*As he starts off Left followed by* SZABUNIEWICZ *carrying most of the suitcases.*) . . . Szabuniewicz, child, help me change. Marianne, please to bring suitcase.

MARIANNE. (*She takes suitcase and starts off then suddenly stops.*) Monsieur Jacobowsky, may I ask you a personal question?

JACOBOWSKY. Anything dear lady.

MARIANNE. Your initials, S. L., what do they stand for?

JACOBOWSKY. Nothing. A proud father's gift when I was born. I will tell you some day, I promise.

MARIANNE. I'll hold you to that. Good night, friend.

JACOBOWSKY. Are we friends?

MARIANNE. Don't you know that? Men are so naive sometimes. We've been friends for ages. Goodnight.

JACOBOWSKY. (*As she exits.*) Goodnight, dear lady. (*She is gone and he repeats the word as the MUSIC comes up.*) Goodnight. (*And he sits on back of wagon as he begins to sing.*)

. . . MARIANNE
DON'T TALK OF SILVER OR VIOLET OR YELLOW
FOR YOU'VE NEVER MET MARIANNE

AND SO THE ONE THING I'M POSITIVE OF IS
THAT GOD MADE ME ONE LUCKY MAN
GENTLEMEN SORRY . . . YOU WON'T KNOW WHAT
    LOVE IS
UNTIL YOU HAVE LOVED MARIANNE!

(*BACK OF WAGON starts off through this, LIGHTS fade, the last thing we see is* JACOBOWSKY's *smiling face as we come up on* . . .

ACT ONE

SCENE 5

OPEN SPOT IN COUNTRYSIDE just outside city of Rennes. MAN WITH SUITCASE *comes out of wagon and crosses Right with* MME. MANZONI, *the carnival owner, chasing after him.*

MAN WITH SUITCASE. (*Hungarian.*) . . . Ha kedved van a Nemeteket kivarni maradjal, de en ebbol ki akarok maradni!

MME. MANZONI. Tegyava! Nemtudom a showt egyedul aloadni, nem hagyhatsz it egyedul!

MARIANNE. (*Coming out of wagon carrying hatbox.*) What's the matter, Mme. Manzoni?

MME. MANZONI. Matter? Just because he hears there are Germans up ahead, he runs off! What about the rest of us, without him there is no show! Hugo the Hungarian Hercules. Hungarian Humbug!

MARIANNE. Are we far from St. Nazaire?

MME. MANZONI. About halfway. Just outside of Rennes. But Monsieur Jacobowsky says you are not to worry, he has gone off with Monsieur Szabuniewicz to find some other means of transportation. I am sorry, Mademoiselle . . . (*As she starts off.*) Oh, the coward! The wretch.

MARIANNE. (*When* MME. MANZONI *is gone, suddenly remembering.*) . . . The papers, I haven't finished sewing them in my hat! (*Calling.*) Tadeusz, dear, would you bring the papers please. And the needle and thread in my straw basket. (*She starts to take hat out of box as* COLONEL *comes out of wagon Left. He wears the shabby suit* JACOBOWSKY *gave him and is quite uncomfortable. Suddenly he takes military cap from behind his back and puts it on.* MARIANNE *looks at him and shakes her head.*) . . . Tadeusz.

COLONEL. (*Angrily tossing cap aside.*) But in these clothes I am not me! I feel like dog, like worm, like everybody else in world.

MARIANNE. Monsieur Jacobowsky says there is a time to advance and a time to retreat . . .

COLONEL. Please, I beg you not to quote to me Monsieur Jacobowsky. If I have to govern myself with his mentality, I'd rather die!

MARIANNE. Monsieur Jacobowsky says it is easy to die but to live requires ingenuity.

COLONEL. Again we quote Monsieur Jacobowsky! That is because you spend all day laughing with him. Then when I come you stop. He loves you, this Monsieur Jacobowsky!

MARIANNE. Ridiculous, what an idea. Do you think so? Oh, it's touching.

COLONEL. So, is how I suspect, you prefer him to me! Very well, for gentleman is only one honorable way to deal with rival; I kill him.

MARIANNE. (*Treating it as a joke.*) You can't kill Monsieur Jacobowsky, he adores you. There, done! Oh, look at that shoulder. (*Putting hat in box and crossing to* COLONEL.) . . . Stand still and let me mend it. (*As she does so.*) He just wants you to love him. He wants the whole world to love him.

COLONEL. In this he will never succeed.

MARIANNE. He knows that. And how cheerful he is about it! In the midst of this frantic journey, he still finds time to make me laugh.

COLONEL. To make you laugh at me!

MARIANNE. At all of us! There . . . (*She has finished mending his coat.*) Shoulder better?

COLONEL. Shoulder better. Heart wounded!

MARIANNE. Poor heart. I'll mend that too.

COLONEL. (*Tragic.*) You don't mend, you break.

MARIANNE. I would never break your heart, Tadeusz, it means too much to me.

COLONEL. You swear on bible? *Correct* bible?

MARIANNE. I swear.

COLONEL. Then I am able for anything! I fight for you, I move mountains for you . . . (*An inspiration.*) I replace Monsieur Jacobowsky for you! You spend all time talking with him because he make you laugh, well from now on *I* make you laugh! (*Desperately.*) Now all I have to do is think of something funny to say.

MARIANNE. Oh, darling, don't try to be like Monsieur Jacobowsky! You have your style and he has his and I love you both.

COLONEL. So, you *do* love him! My course is clear, we fight.

MARIANNE. (*Shaking her head.*) It's true, you *are* a fifteenth century man. (*Before* COLONEL *can speak.*) . . . And yes, I got that from Monsieur Jacobowsky too!

JACOBOWSKY. (*Entering excitedly at that moment followed by* SZABUNIEWICZ, *parcels hidden behind their backs.*) Mademoiselle Marianne, you'll never believe who I met in Rennes; my brother-in-law's cousin from Leipzig! Now he's headwaiter at the best cafe in town and for old times' sake, and my watch chain, he let us have some very interesting commodities.

MARIANNE. (*As they reveal parcels.*) Food!

SZABUNIEWICZ. Sausage, bread, cheese, even knife and fork!

JACOBOWSKY. Mademoiselle Marianne, have you ever been to Chez Maxim?

MARIANNE. I passed it once on a trip to Paris but I never dared go in.

JACOBOWSKY. Today we dare! (*Folding napkin over his arm and crossing to* COLONEL *who stands stiffly to one side.*) . . . Right this way M'sieur, 'Dame. Your table is ready. Colonel, will you follow me?

COLONEL. (*Drawing himself up.*) I am sorry but I not hungry. (*Starting Left.*) . . . Come, Szabuniewicz!

SZABUNIEWICZ. But I hungry.

COLONEL. When Colonel not hungry, you not hungry!

SZABUNIEWICZ. (*Following him.*) I not hungry.

JACOBOWSKY. (*As MUSIC comes up and he opens imaginary menu.*) Now, Mademoiselle, may I suggest the caviar, to begin with, "nature" of course with just a bit of lemon, then the loup en croute, wait till you taste that croute, followed by just the tiniest soupçon of . . . (*As he takes tablecloth from basket and starts to tree stump Right.*) Let me check with the kitchen.

MARIANNE. (*As through this* JACOBOWSKY *sets table, serves sausage and cheese as if it was pheasant, pours water as if it were champagne.*)
ISN'T HE WITTY?
DOESN'T HE MAKE YOU SMILE?
HE'S CLEVER AND RESILIENT
HAVEN'T YOU NOTICED
HIS CONTINENTAL STYLE
HIS REPARTEE IS BRILLIANT
HIS SENSE OF HONOR
HIS SENSE OF HUMOR
HIS SENSE OF ORDER AND PLAN
POET AND PREACHER
SCHOLAR AND TEACHER
MY LITTLE RENAISSANCE MAN!
SO MUCH POTENTIAL
HE HAS TO STILL EXPLORE
A GENIE IN A BOTTLE
IF THEY WOULD LISTEN
HE COULD RESOLVE THE WAR
MY POLISH ARISTOTLE

HIS ALLURE
HIS CHARM AND HIS CANDOR
MAKE THIS TOUR
SEEM GRANDER AND GRANDER
MOMENT TO MOMENT
I LIKE HIM MORE AND MORE!

COLONEL. (*With mounting anger as MUSIC continues.*) Loup en croute, cousins-in-law from Leipzig, Chez Maxim! (*And he bursts out.*)

LESS AND LESS
I LIKE THIS JACOBOWSKY
MY CONTEMPT
THIS FELLOW IS BENEATH
MORE AND MORE
THOSE IRRITATING WAYS OF HIS
THAT SUGAR COATED GLAZE OF HIS
IS ROTTING MY BACK TEETH
HE GIVES ME INDIGESTION
WHEN HE SMILES
HE AGGRAVATES MY SINUS
WHEN HE LAUGHS
HE GIVES ME NERVOUS STRESS
SHE THINKS HE'S CUDDLY AS A PUP
I THINK I'M GOING TO THROW UP
MORE AND MORE
I LIKE HIM LESS AND LESS!

(*Suddenly* JACOBOWSKY *gets carried away and still with napkin folded over his arm seizes* MARIANNE *in his arms and pivots her into tango poses as the* COLONEL *paces furiously and they sing.*)

MARIANNE.	COLONEL.
ISN'T HE WITTY,	LESS AND LESS
DOESN'T HE MAKE YOU SMILE?	I LIKE THIS JACOBOWSKY
HE'S CLEVER AND RESILIENT	MY CONTEMPT
HAVEN'T YOU NOTICED HIS CONTINENTAL STYLE?	THE FELLOW IS BENEATH
HIS REPARTEE IS BRILLIANT	MORE AND MORE
	THOSE IRRITATING WAYS OF HIS
	THAT SUGAR COATED GLAZE OF HIS

HIS SENSE OF HONOR,
HIS SENSE OF HUMOR
HIS SENSE OF ORDER
    AND PLAN
POET AND PREACHER,
SCHOLAR AND TEACHER
MY LITTLE RENAISSANCE
    MAN!
SO MUCH POTENTIAL
HE HAS TO STILL
    EXPLORE
A GENIE IN A BOTTLE
IF THEY WOULD LISTEN
HE COULD RESOLVE THE
    WAR
MY POLISH ARISTOTLE
HIS ALLURE,
HIS CHARM AND HIS
    CANDOR
MAKE THIS TOUR
SEEM GRANDER AND
    GRANDER
MOMENT TO MOMENT
I LIKE HIM MORE AND
    MORE!

IS ROTTING BY BACK
    TEETH
HE GIVES ME
    INDIGESTION
WHEN HE SMILES
HE AGGRAVATES MY
    SINUS
WHEN HE LAUGHS
HE GIVES ME NERVOUS
    STRESS
SHE THINKS HE'S
    CUDDLY
AS A PUP
I THINK I'M GOING
TO THROW UP
MORE AND MORE
I LIKE HIM LESS AND
    LESS

(*MUSIC continues as* JACOBOWSKY *and* MARIANNE *dance a wild
    tango. Even* SZABUNIEWICZ *becomes part of it as the*
    COLONEL's *fury mounts and mounts.*)

MARIANNE.
MY POLISH ARISTOTLE
HIS ALLURE,
HIS CHARM AND CANDOR
MAKE THIS TOUR
SEEM GRANDER AND
    GRANDER
MOMENT TO MOMENT
I LIKE HIM MORE AND
    MORE!
MOMENT TO MOMENT
I LIKE HIM MORE AND
    MORE!

COLONEL.
SHE THINKS HE'S
    CUDDLY
AS A PUP
I THINK I'M GOING
TO THROW UP
MORE AND MORE
I LIKE HIM LESS AND
    LESS!
MORE AND MORE
I LIKE HIM LESS AND
    LESS!

(*End SONG,* MARIANNE *and* JACOBOWSKY *are laughing together as* COLONEL *suddenly shouts.*)

COLONEL. . . . Monsieur Jacobowsky, you will step away from that woman at once!

MARIANNE. Tadeusz, I will *not* have this shouting! Monsieur Jacobowsky has behaved like a gentleman and I insist you treat him as such.

COLONEL. Very well, I treat him like a gentleman. S. L. Jacobowsky, I challenge you to a duel! Szabuniewicz, child, pistols!

SZABUNIEWICZ. (*Who has gone over to picnic, now hastily eating.*) In a minute, I just finishing lunch.

COLONEL. (*A roar.*) Szabuniewicz!

SZABUNIEWICZ. (*Choking.*) Swallow opp whole egg!

JACOBOWSKY. (*As* SZABUNIEWICZ *goes to get pistols.*) Colonel, I am honored to be treated like a gentleman and challenged to a duel but do you think this is the proper time for such a distinction? It might be wiser to spend our energies getting to the coast.

COLONEL. Words, excuses! Jacobowsky, you are afraid of me!

JACOBOWSKY. Yes, Colonel. Very much.

COLONEL. Well, to tell the truth, I am afraid of you! I am afraid of the thoughts that you have that only she can share, the laughter that dries up when I come near. Fight you I must, Jacobowsky, to prove I can conquer fear. Because if I fear, I die.

JACOBOWSKY. But to prove this to yourself I'll probably have to die.

COLONEL. Perhaps you will kill me. You are a small man, Jacobowsky. By fighting you, I give you stature. What Nazis take away from you, I, Stjerbinsky, give you back . . . (*To* SZABUNIEWICZ.) Marianne, you will please step aside.

JACOBOWSKY. (*With sudden determination.*) Why not? What if I do kill him? It's possible. In my veins flows the blood of great fathers, David, Saul . . . And the truth is you are right, Colonel, I am in love with her. I am happy to say the words for once. I am happy to hear the words for once. I love her! I love her! I love her! (*A roar.*) . . . Szabuniewicz, child, pistols!

MARIANNE. (*Shaking her head.*) In the middle of the great war, this little war. What hope is there for the world?

JACOBOWSKY. (*As* SZABUNIEWICZ *helps* COLONEL *off with his coat.*) Wait! Szabuniewicz is your second, who is mine?

MARIANNE. (*Involuntarily.*) I am! (*Taking off her scarf.*) . . . Monsieur Jacobowsky, I have no token. Will this do?

JACOBOWSKY. (*Taking scarf.*) Now I *must* survive!

COLONEL. Jacobowsky, prepare to meet your maker!

JACOBOWSKY. I have been since I was five. May He have mercy on both our souls.

COLONEL. Ten steps, then we fire.

JACOBOWSKY. Five!

COLONEL. Very well, Monsieur.

SZABUNIEWICZ. Ready, gentlemen?

JACOBOWSKY/COLONEL. Ready!

SZABUNIEWICZ. One. Two. Three. Four . . .

(*Through this an* S.S. CAPTAIN *and* TWO SOLDIERS *have suddenly appeared Upstage Center.*)

S.S. CAPTAIN. Halt! Who are you? What is going on here?

COLONEL. What it look like is going on!

S.S. CAPTAIN. What did you say?

JACOBOWSKY. (*Imitating accent.*) He said what it look like is going on? We are rehearsing!

S.S. CAPTAIN. Rehearsing?

JACOBOWSKY. Our sharpshooting act. We are all artists with the world-famous Carnival Manzoni. May I present myself, Hugo the Hungarian Hercules. This is my partner the lovely Mademoiselle Marianne, and these are the two clowns who assist us, Bobo and Toto.

COLONEL. (*To* SZABUNIEWICZ.) Who he call Bobo?

S.S. CAPTAIN. *You* are the Hungarian Hercules?

JACOBOWSKY. Of course. (*As* MME. MANZONI *enters.*) . . . Madame Manzoni, I was just telling these gentlemen about our performance tonight in which I, the Hungarian Hercules, will do my sharpshooting act assisted by Mademoiselle Marianne and Bobo and Toto.

COLONEL. Why he look at me when he say Bobo?

MME. MANZONI. (*Seeing what* JACOBOWSKY *is up to.*) Don't tell me you haven't heard of the great Hugo, Captain! The finest sharpshooter in Europe, the human cannonball . . .

COLONEL. I no Bobo!

JACOBOWSKY. (*Imitating him.*) I no Bobo! Isn't he amusing, the children adore him. Now be quiet, you great oaf, or you'll give the show away.

S.S. CAPTAIN. Madame, your Hungarian Hercules has intrigued me. What time does the performance begin?

MME. MANZONI. At eight, Captain, but . . .

S.S. CAPTAIN. You will reserve a place for me tonight. Captain

Meuller. (*To* JACOBOWSKY.) . . . And, Monsieur Hercules, I expect to see all I have been promised. *Including* the cannon. (*As he looks at* COLONEL.) I no Bobo! (*And he laughs. Then, in German, to* SOLDIERS *as they start off.*) . . . Come along! On the double!

MARIANNE. (*The moment they are gone.*) Monsieur Jacobowsky, we must run!

JACOBOWSKY. In broad daylight? We wouldn't get ten meters. And we couldn't do that to Madame Manzoni; if the Germans find out she lied to them, they'd arrest her.

SZABUNIEWICZ. So what we do?

MME. MANZONI. Do? The show! (*Calling.*) . . . Madame Lillian, bring the Hungarian Hercules' costume!

(MME. LILLIAN *and* VARIOUS OTHER PERFORMERS *start in as we come up on* . . .

ACT ONE

SCENE 6

Dressing area of carnival.

MME. LILLIAN. . . . Coming, coming! (*Holding oversized human cannonball costume against him.*) I'll have to take the chest in a little.

LION TAMER. No need to worry about the cannon, Monsieur Jacobowsky. Getting in's the only tricky part; getting out takes care of itself.

FAT WOMAN. One little hint. Do not get in head first.

STRONG MAN. And you needn't worry about the boom. By the time you hear it you'll be miles away.

MME. MANZONI. (*As* JACOBOWSKY *begins to totter.*) Out all of you! The Grand Parade begins in ten minutes! (JACOBOWSKY *sits weakly.*) . . . Monsieur Jacobowsky, what's the matter?

JACOBOWSKY. Everything, Madame Manzoni. All my life, no matter what I had to face, I felt that with God's help I was equal to the situation. But there's a limit to how much divine intervention one can ask for.

MME. MANZONI. Then trust yourself, Monsieur Jacobowsky! A man can do anything he chooses if he has the right reason. (*And she crosses herself as she exits.*)

JACOBOWSKY. (*Touching* MARIANNE's *scarf.*) I have the right rea-

son. (*And he looks at himself in the dressing table mirror as he sings.*)
WALK THE HIGHEST WIRE
DO ONE EXTRAORDINARY THING
JUMP THE RING OF FIRE
DO ONE EXTRAORDINARY THING
MAKE THE CROWD APPLAUD THE SKILL AND THE
     DARING
OF THE FRIGHTENED FELLOW IN THE MAIN RING
THOUGH YOU MAY ADMIRE
WHAT OTHER MIGHTY MEN HAVE DONE
YOU TOP THEM ALL WHEN YOU DO ONE
EXTRAORDINARY THING
     (*Tempo begins as* JACOBOWSKY *continues with mounting
     confidence.*)
MAKE THE MOUNTAIN MOVE
DO ONE EXTRAORDINARY THING
LIFE'S WORTH MORE WHEN YOU'VE
DONE ONE EXTRAORDINARY THING
REACH THE FARTHEST SPOT OUT ON THE HORIZON
MAKE YOUR WILDEST DREAMS WAKE UP AND TAKE
     WING
YOU CAN ALWAYS PROVE
YOU'VE EARNED YOUR MOMENT IN THE SUN
WHEN YOU CAN PROUDLY POINT TO ONE
EXTRAORDINARY THING!

(*Scene expands to include* MARIANNE, SZABUNIEWICZ, *and the*
     COLONEL, *as they dress for the performance and catch the
     excitement of the moment.*)

MARIANNE.
WHEN YOUR STRENGTH IS FAILING AND YOU CAN'T
     CONTINUE
USE THAT POWER YOU DON'T EVEN KNOW IS IN
     YOU
JACOBOWSKY/MARIANNE/COLONEL/SZABUNIEWICZ.
YOU CAN ALWAYS PROVE
YOU'VE EARNED YOUR MOMENT IN THE SUN
WHEN YOU CAN PROUDLY POINT TO ONE
EXTRAORDINARY THING!

(*By now* Jacobowsky, Marianne, Colonel *and* Szabuniewicz
    have exited as Other Performers, *costumed for the Grand
    Parade, start on and we go to* . . .

ACT ONE

Scene 7

THE MIDWAY OF CARNIVAL MANZONI, that evening.

Various Performers.
WE GO OUR DREARY WAYS
AND THINK THAT LIFE'S COMPLETE
WE LIVE OUR HUMDRUM DAYS
AND THEN RETIRE

BUT IF YOU DO INSTEAD
ONE INCANDESCENT FEAT
YOU'LL ALWAYS HOLD YOUR HEAD
A LITTLE HIGHER
A LITTLE HIGHER . . .
    Mme. Manzoni/All Performers. (*As Grand Parade begins.*)
CHANGE TOMORROW'S COURSE
DO ONE EXTRAORDINARY THING
WITH INHUMAN FORCE
DO ONE EXTRAORDINARY THING
SAIL THE SKIES AND PLUMB THE DEPTHS OF THE
    OCEAN
THRILL THE WORLD AND MAKE THE UNIVERSE SING
HAVE NO GREAT REMORSE
FOR ALL THE DEEDS YOU'VE NEVER DONE
AS LONG AS YOU ACCOMPLISH ONE
EXTRAORDINARY THING . . .

(*The* Band *blares forth as the Grand Parade circles the stage with*
    Performers *tumbling, leaping, whirling.* DANCE *section ends
    as they sing.*)

All Performers.
CATCH THE WINNING BALL
DO ONE EXTRAORDINARY THING

SCALE THE CASTLE WALL
DO ONE EXTRAORDINARY THING
SLAY THE DRAGON FOR THE HAND OF THE PRINCESS
BRING THE FLAG OF VICT'RY BACK TO THE KING
NEVER ENVY ALL
THE RACES OTHER PEOPLE RUN
THE CROWN IS YOURS FOR DOING ONE
EXTRAORDINARY THING
ONE EXTRAORDINARY . . .

(*The blast of a whistle, and* MME. MANZONI *steps forward.*)

MME. MANZONI. (*Over sting in MUSIC as* MARIANNE *comes out with brace of pistols followed by* TWO CARNIVAL PEOPLE *carrying target with silhouette of man surrounded by colored balloons.*) And now, ladies and gentlemen, the Carnival Manzoni is proud to present the most dazzling display of death-defying marksmanship the world has ever seen!

(SZABUNIEWICZ *starts out, sees target, starts immediately off then is stopped and put into place against the target as* JACOBOWSKY, *in his sharpshooter costume, makes his entrance. He crosses to* MARIANNE, *puts on his glasses, then takes the first pistol and with his hand trembling, aims it at* SZABUNIEWICZ. *He pulls the trigger, the first balloon pops, both he and* SZABUNIEWICZ *heave a sigh of relief, and the act continues. He shoots the last balloon—dangerously placed between* SZABUNIEWICZ' *legs—a triumphant fanfare and he exits as* SZABUNIEWICZ, *half-fainting, exits behind him.* MME. MANZONI *has started forward through this, sting in MUSIC, as she announces.*)

MME. MANZONI. For children of all ages, the delightful Bobo!

(*And the* COLONEL *start on in an outrageous costume made up of several inflated inner tubes covered by a huge clown's costume. He falls, bounces up again, his* TWO GIRL ASSISTANTS *run against him and bounce off, etc.* S.S. CAPTAIN *has wandered suspiciously by through this and* COLONEL *bounces merrily against him.*)

COLONEL. (*Now completely caught up in the spirit of the performance.*) I Bobo! (COLONEL *suddenly falls, is unable to rise, his feet* helplessly wave in air. The FULL COMPANY comes to his aid as they sing.)

FULL COMPANY. (As COLONEL is helped up and led off.)
WHEN YOUR STRENGTH IS FALLING AND YOU CAN'T
    CONTINUE
USE THAT POWER YOU DON'T EVEN KNOW IS IN
    YOU

MAKE THE MOUNTAIN MOVE
DO ONE EXTRAORDINARY THING
LIFE'S WORTH MORE WHEN YOU'VE
DONE ONE EXTRAORDINARY THING
REACH THE FARTHEST SPOT OUT ON THE HORIZON
MAKE YOUR WILDEST DREAMS WAKE UP AND TAKE
    WING
YOU CAN ALWAYS PROVE
YOU'VE EARNED YOUR MOMENT IN THE SUN
WHEN YOU CAN PROUDLY POINT TO ONE
EXTRAORDINARY THING!
MAKE THE MOUNTAIN MOVE
CHANGE TOMORROW'S COURSE
AH!

(Through last of this JACOBOWSKY has come out in his human can-
    nonball costume and is lifted up as the number ends. A whistle
    and MME. MANZONI makes the announcement.)

MME. MANZONI. (As JACOBOWSKY parades back and forth show-
ing off his cape and a huge cannon starts on Stage Right.) . . . And
now, the star attraction of the Carnival Manzoni, Hugo the Hungarian Hercules, who will descend into the mouth of a loaded cannon
. . . not head first . . . from which his partner Mademoiselle
Marianne will fire a charge equivalent to twenty kilos of TNT thus
propelling him forth at a velocity of over 200 kilometers per hour!
Ladies and gentlemen, the Human Cannonball!

(JACOBOWSKY is loaded into the cannon by TWO ASSISTANTS when
    suddenly a VOICE calls out.)

S.S. CAPTAIN. Halte! (Crossing to JACOBOWSKY whose head
sticks out of mouth of cannon.) . . . Before the Hungarian
Hercules attempts this daring feat, there is one question I should like

to ask him. In his native language, of course. (*In Hungarian.*)
Honnet jottel Magyarorszagbol, miota vagy Franciaorszagba?

JACOBOWSKY. (*After a pause, turning front.*) Seven languages
. . . but no Hungarian. (*As he disappears into the cannon.*) . . .
Marianne, quick! The fuse!

S.S. CAPTAIN. (*To* SOLDIERS *as* MARIANNE *starts to cannon.*)
Halte sie.

MARIANNE. (*As she grapples with* SOLDIERS.) Tadeusz, help!

COLONEL. (*Pushing his way through* CROWD *and pulling*
SOLDIERS *from* MARIANNE.) I am coming, my life!

S.S. CAPTAIN. Halte sie, berlung. Verhaften sie, Verhaften sie!

(*Melee, screams,* MARIANNE *runs to cannon and touches off fuse. A
blast, dummy shoots off Left, shots, shouts,* CARNIVAL PEOPLE
and SOLDIERS *rushing across stage. Lights change, shots and
shouts grow fainter,* LAST SOLDIER *runs off and there is silence.*
ONE *or* TWO CARNIVAL PEOPLE *scurry across with their suitcases then, after a moment,* MARIANNE, COLONEL *and*
SZABUNIEWICZ *start cautiously on from Right. Another few
seconds and* JACOBOWSKY *joins them.*)

JACOBOWSKY. . . . We're in luck! A man with a truck hauling
nets to the coast. He can take two but I persuaded him that with a
little crowding space could be made for the three of you. But you
must hurry!

MARIANNE. But what about you, Monsieur Jacobowsky?

JACOBOWSKY. There is no boat waiting for me in St. Nazaire, I
must head south to Spain while there is still time.

COLONEL. But Germans in south! Is not honorable to abandon you
now.

JACOBOWSKY. And would it be honorable to have the names of all
those men fighting for a free Poland fall into the hands of the Nazis?
Now hurry or the truck won't wait!

COLONEL. (*Realizing the truth of it.*) He is right, we have no
choice. (*As he starts Left.*) . . . Come, Szabuniewicz! Marianne.

MARIANNE. (*Torn, taking his hand.*) Dear Monsieur Jacobowsky,
I will not forget you. And we will see each other again, I know it!

JACOBOWSKY. Then I have a memory and a hope. I thank you for
both.

MARIANNE. (*As she exits.*) Goodbye, dear friend!

JACOBOWSKY. Goodbye, dear lady! (*Then softly as he waves.*)
. . . Goodbye. (*As we hear the sound of a truck starting off. His*

waving subsides, loneliness descends on him. Then he pulls himself out of it and bends down to pick up his jacket. Suddenly he stops, for under his coat is MARIANNE's *hatbox. He picks it up, looks inside.*) Oh my God, that schlemiel has forgotten the papers! (*Shaking his head.*) . . . What a joke! I, the only son of Reba Jacobowsky, hold in my hands the future of Poland! (*As he rises.*) What must I do? Deliver it to him! But if the Nazis catch me with these, it's goodbye S. L. Jacobowsky . . . (*Holding hat.*) But I'll see you again, Marianne! I'll see you again! (*And he sings.*)
REACH THE FARTHEST SPOT OUT ON THE HORIZON
MAKE YOUR WILDEST DREAMS WAKE UP AND TAKE
   WING
   (*A shout as he picks up jacket and briefcase.*)
I'LL SEE YOU AGAIN!
   (*Starting after them.*)
YOU CAN ALWAYS PROVE
YOU'VE EARNED YOUR MOMENT IN THE SUN . . .

(*MUSIC continues as* JACOBOWSKY *goes off Left and CURTAIN comes down on* . . .

END OF ACT ONE

ACT TWO

Scene 1

*Near end of ENTR'ACTE we come up on COUNTRYSIDE SOME-
WHERE IN WEST OF FRANCE. It is pre-dawn and through the
morning mist we see* TWO GERMAN SOLDIERS *Down Right as
barge starts slowly on Left to Right.*

FIRST SOLDIER. (*Shouting.*) You! Where are you going?

BARGEMAN'S VOICE. (*Still off.*) To St. Nazaire!

SECOND SOLDIER. Carrying what?

BARGEMAN'S VOICE. Vegetables. Potatoes, leeks, spinach. Some
strawberries.

FIRST SOLDIER. You may continue.

BARGEMAN. (*Appearing as* SOLDIERS *start off.*) Thank you,
Monsieur. (*A moment, then* BARGEMAN *addresses someone in
bow.*) . . . You can come out now, they're gone.

JACOBOWSKY. (*Appearing from beneath vegetables.*) Do you suppose we'll be stopped again?

BARGEMAN. I shouldn't think so. No roads cross the canal for
three hours at least. Why don't you get some sleep?

JACOBOWSKY. With so much spinning around in my head?
Impossible!

BARGEMAN. The Germans?

JACOBOWSKY. Not exactly. Something that even my dear mother,
wise woman that she was, didn't prepare me for . . . (*As MUSIC
comes up.*) A third possibility. (BARGEMAN *shakes his head and exits
as sun comes slowly up and* JACOBOWSKY *sings.*)

SEE THAT LOVELY LADY IN THE LIVING ROOM
LIGHTING UP THE EVENING WITH HER YOUTHFUL
    BLOOM
FROM HER GRACEFUL PRESENCE YOU MAY WELL
    PRESUME
THAT'S MRS. S. L. JACOBOWSKY

I'LL READ HER MY SPINOZA AND MY BAUDILAIRE
WALK HER THROUGH TUILERIES TO GET SOME AIR
EVERYTHING I USED TO DO ALONE I'LL SHARE

WITH MRS. S. L. JACOBOWSKY
WE'LL ARTFULLY COMBINE
HER OLD WORLD WITH MINE
AND WE'LL HANG A CRUCIFIX IN ONE ROOM
A MEZZUZAH IN THE SUN ROOM

IF REBA JACOBOWSKY COULD LOOK DOWN AND SEE
THIS MIRACLE OF MIRACLES THAT'S COME TO ME
SHE'D GLADLY HAVE A SHIKSA IN THE FAMILY
A GIRL WHO'LL BRING SUCH MAGIC TO MY LIFE
I'LL GO TO MASS AND I'LL RESPECT HER WISHES
AND SHE'LL START USING SEPARATE DISHES
WHEN MRS. JACOBOWSKY IS MY WIFE

THOUGH OTHER WIVES MAY NEVER GET THEIR
     HOUSEWORK DONE
THOUGH OTHER WIVES MAY BAKE A TART THAT
     WEIGHS A TON
WITH HER THE POSSIBILITIES ARE ONLY ONE
A PERFECT MRS. JACOBOWSKY

I WILL NOT QUESTION WHY
I AM BLINDED BY
ONE SWEET SMILE THAT HARDLY NEEDS
     CORRECTION
HOW CAN YOU CORRECT PERFECTION?

AND WHEN IT'S ALMOST OVER AND I'M GRAY AND
     BENT
TRYING TO REMEMBER WHERE THE YEARS ALL
     WENT
TRYING TO RECALL HOW MUCH EACH MOMENT
     MEANT
AND LOOKING FOR THE MEANING OF MY LIFE
WHEN NOT A SOUL REMEMBERS WHAT MY NAME IS
MY ONE LASTING CLAIM TO FAME IS
THAT MRS. JACOBOWSKY WAS MY WIFE!

(*SONG ends with* JACOBOWSKY, *bathed in sunlight, seated on back
     of barge as it disappears Off Right and we come up on* . . .

ACT TWO

SCENE 2

THE CAFE OF PAPA CLAIRON AT ST. NAZAIRE. At rise PAPA
CLAIRON, CLAUDINE, *the waitress,* VARIOUS PATRONS, *are
scurrying about setting up chairs, tables, lights, etc. as* MAN
WITH FLOWER IN HIS BUTTONHOLE *comes crisply on.*

MAN WITH FLOWER. . . . What time is it, Monsieur Clairon?

PAPA CLAIRON. (*Checking his watch.*) Nearly seven.

MAN WITH FLOWER. Where *is* that colonel, the boat sails at ten!

PAPA CLAIRON. Patience, he still has three hours. Come on, have
a drink . . .

BRIDE'S MOTHER. (*Coming in followed by* SEVERAL PEOPLE *as*
PAPA CLAIRON *leads* MAN WITH FLOWER *to bar.*) . . . I am sorry
but the answer is no.

BRIDE'S AUNT. But Thérèse . . .

BRIDE'S MOTHER. You are her aunt, I am her mother, the answer
is no!

BRIDE'S FATHER. Thérèse, I beg you, give in! The whole country
has given in, why won't you?

BRIDE'S MOTHER. (*As cafe door opens and* JACOBOWSKY, *carrying hatbox, starts in.*) For the last time *no!*

JACOBOWSKY. (*To* MAN *hurrying by with chairs.*) Excuse me, is
this the cafe of Papa Clairon?

MAN. It is, Monsieur, but he's busy now.

JACOBOWSKY. (*To* WAITRESS.) I'm looking for a party of three;
they are to meet a man with a flower in his buttonhole . . .

CLAUDINE. In a moment, Monsieur, I must fix the garlands.

JACOBOWSKY. (*To* YOUNG MAN *on ladder hanging lanterns.*) He
will offer them a drink, they will say To Liberty!, two men and a
beautiful young woman. Also a bird, Lulu!

YOUNG MAN. Birds, no. Beautiful women we have lots. (*Indicating* GIRL IN WHITE DRESS *as he moves ladder.*) . . . Only not that
one, she's mine.

JACOBOWSKY. (*To* BRIDE'S MOTHER.) Madame, I am looking for a
man with a flower.

BRIDE'S MOTHER. Pardon, Monsieur, but the bride's mother has
no time for lost men with flowers when she can't even find a rabbi for
her only daughter's wedding!

JACOBOWSKY. You're having a wedding *now?*

BRIDE'S MOTHER. A wedding yes; a wedding with a rabbi, maybe. The only one we had in St. Nazaire left yesterday and the groom didn't make up his mind till today. (*She glares at the* YOUNG MAN *hanging lanterns who shrugs sheepishly then hurries on.*)

BRIDE'S FATHER. (*To* BRIDE'S MOTHER.) Perhaps it would be wiser to have a civil ceremony, Thérèse. They say the Germans are just across the Loire.

BRIDE'S MOTHER. Just because the barbarians are at the gates is no reason to compromise! I heard the words and I want my daughter to hear the words.

JACOBOWSKY. They *are* very moving. (*He recites in Hebrew.*) . . . The Lord bless thee, and keep thee; The Lord make His face to shine upon thee . . . (. . . *Ye-vaw-re-he-haw adoshem ve-yeesh-me-re-haw. Yaw-air adoshem paw-nov ay-leh-haw* . . .)

BRIDE'S MOTHER. Monsieur, you are not by any chance . . .

JACOBOWSKY. Alas, no, Madame. My father was a student of Biblical history and odd bits of learning rubbed off.

BRIDE'S FATHER. Half a loaf is better than none, Thérèse!

BRIDE'S MOTHER. I'm not sure that goes for half a rabbi. (*After a moment.*) . . . Very well, you will read the ceremony.

JACOBOWSKY. But it won't be legal!

BRIDE'S MOTHER. If you say the words and they believe them, in God's eyes it's legal.

JACOBOWSKY. But . . .

BRIDE'S MOTHER. (*Shaking his hand.*) Done! I'll tell the others.

JACOBOWSKY. But the papers . . .

BRIDE'S FATHER. (*Turning around to reveal flower he has just received from* CLAUDINE *in his buttonhole.*) I have them right here, the marriage certificate, the dowry . . .

JACOBOWSKY. (*Seeing only the flower.*) Thank God! (*Embracing him.*) . . . I've been looking for you everywhere.

BRIDE'S FATHER. We just saw each other a minute ago.

JACOBOWSKY. That was before I knew who you were! (*And he sings.*)

WHAT A LOVELY BOUTONNIERE YOU'RE WEARING
IT SHOWS SUCH CULTURE, SUCH STYLE AND GRACE
    (*Aside.*)
THE COLONEL WILL BE JOINING US IN JUST A LITTLE
    WHILE . . .
    BRIDE'S FATHER.
I'LL TELL MY WIFE TO SET AN EXTRA PLACE.

(*As MUSIC continues.*)

. . . Any friend of the rabbi's is always welcome.

JACOBOWSKY. (*Trying to make him understand.*)

HAVE NO FEAR THE LITTLE HAT IS WITH ME
IN MY SAFEKEEPING, AND NO ONE KNOWS

BRIDE'S FATHER.

WE'LL NEED IT FOR THE CEREMONY—IS IT BLACK
      OR WHITE?

JACOBOWSKY.

IT'S BEIGE, AND HAS A VEIL AND LITTLE BOWS.

BRIDE'S FATHER. Oh, a reform rabbi! Well, come along, Monsieur . . .

JACOBOWSKY.

AREN'T YOU GOING TO OFFER ME SOMETHING
SO THAT THIS MISSION WON'T FAIL?

BRIDE'S FATHER.

OF COURSE, MY FRIEND, WOULD YOU PREFER CASH
OR SHOULD I PUT A CHECK IN THE MAIL?

JACOBOWSKY. (*By now a bit desperate.*)

SUDDENLY I'M FEELING AWFULLY THIRSTY
PERHAPS A COGNAC MY GRACIOUS HOST
I'D LIKE TO DRINK TO LIBERTY! TO LIBERTY, MY
      FRIENDS!

BRIDE'S FATHER.

NOW THAT'S A MOST PECULIAR WEDDING TOAST.

. . . Instead, Monsieur,

(*And he sings.*)

SING A SONG OF MAZELTOV
LET YOUR JOY
FILL THE ROOM
SING A SONG OF MAZELTOV
GOOD LUCK, GOOD FORTUNE, AND GOOD CHEER
CLINK YOUR GLASSES TO THE BRIDE
DRINK A TOAST
TO THE GROOM
SING A SONG OF MAZELTOV
MAY LIFE GROW SWEETER EVERY YEAR!
MAZELTOV
AS THIS IMPORTANT MOMENT ARRIVES
MAZELTOV
MAY LAUGHTER ALWAYS RING THROUGH THEIR
      LIVES

(JACOBOWSKY *is about to take the glass from* BRIDE'S FATHER *when he is interrupted by* FOUR MORE GUESTS, *each wearing flower, each holding a drink.*)

MORE GUESTS.
SING A SONG OF MAZELTOV
LET YOUR JOY
FILL THE ROOM
    MORE GUESTS. (*Also with flowers and glasses.*)
SING A SONG OF MAZELTOV
GOOD LUCK, GOOD FORTUNE, AND GOOD CHEER
    MORE GUESTS. (*More flowers, more glasses.*)
CLINK YOUR GLASSES TO THE BRIDE
DRINK A TOAST
TO THE GROOM
SING A SONG OF MAZELTOV
    ALL.
MAY LIFE GROW SWEETER EVERY YEAR!

(*As MUSIC continues and begins to have a slow plaintive beat,* JACOBOWSKY *gets caught up in the age-old strain and almost without realizing it he begins to remove his jacket, his tie and unbutton the top button of his shirt. MUSIC continues and as* WEDDING GUESTS *surround him he begins the slow insistent steps of a traditional wedding dance. DANCE grows in excitement as* ALL GUESTS *join, building to climax as they sing.*)

GUESTS.
SING A SONG OF MAZELTOV
GOOD LUCK, GOOD FORTUNE, AND GOOD CHEER

SING A SONG OF MAZELTOV
MAY LIFE GROW SWEETER EVERY YEAR!

(*End NUMBER, applause as* MAN *suddenly rushes into cafe.*)

MAN. . . . Germans! They've crossed the bridge! You can see the tanks from here!
BRIDE'S MOTHER. But there must be a service! Otherwise it isn't a wedding!
MAN. Have the service, but for God's sake, hurry!

(*And as MUSIC becomes double-time, we do the entire ceremony in forty-five seconds with canopy being put up,* BRIDE *coming down aisle, etc. Suddenly the MUSIC stops with a sting, LIGHTS pour down on* JACOBOWSKY *in skullcap and prayer shawl standing before the* BRIDAL COUPLE, *as in the suspended silence he says the age-old words.*)

JACOBOWSKY.
Ye-va-re-he-haw adoshem ve-yeesh-me-re-haw.
Yaw-air-adoshem paw-nov ay-leh-haw vee-hoo-neh-haw.
Ye-sew adoshem paw-nov ay-ley-haw ve-yow-same le-haw sholom.
Aw-mayn.
(The Lord bless thee, and keep thee;
The Lord make His face to shine upon thee, and be gracious unto thee;
The Lord lift up His countenance upon thee, and give thee peace.)

(*The glass is put on the floor, the* GROOM *steps on it, the* ENTIRE COMPANY *shouts,* "Mazeltov!", *the* BRIDE *and* GROOM *kiss and in even less time than it took to set up, the canopy is dismantled, the lanterns taken down, the flowers removed, and as a heavy pounding is heard at the door, one by one the* WEDDING PARTY *exits. Finally only* JACOBOWSKY, PAPA CLAIRON, CLAUDINE, TWO CUSTOMERS, *and the* MAN WITH FLOWER *remain. Pounding at door has become louder and louder, we hear shouts in German outside, as* DICE PLAYER *takes glass from bar, crosses to* JACOBOWSKY.)

DICE PLAYER. To liberty!
JACOBOWSKY. (*As* PAPA CLAIRON *pushes switch that plunges bar into darkness.*) Mazeltov!

(*A moment of silence then* S.S. CAPTAIN *accompanied by* TWO SOLDIERS *and local* COMMISSAIRE OF POLICE *wearing Nazi armband burst into room.*)

S.S. CAPTAIN. . . . What is going on here! Put on those lights! (*As LIGHTS go on revealing* MAN WITH FLOWER *reading at bar,* JACOBOWSKY *nowhere in sight.*) Who are you?
PAPA CLAIRON. The proprietor, Monsieur. My name is Clairon. These are my friends.

S.S. CAPTAIN. (*To* FIRST SOLDIER.) Check their papers. (*Back to* CLAIRON.) . . . There was noise when our car pulled up. Music.

PAPA CLAIRON. We were singing. Our Claudine has just become engaged and we were celebrating.

S.S. CAPTAIN. How the ear plays tricks. From outside it sounded like a dozen voices at least. (*In German.*) . . . Klaus upstairs, Werner the cellar, you the washroom. (*In English.*) And who is this gentleman?

(*Without looking up from his book,* MAN WITH FLOWER *takes out passport, hands it to* COMMISSAIRE *who opens it.*)

COMMISSAIRE. A special diplomatic passport. From the Armistice Commission in Wiesbaden.

S.S. CAPTAIN. My congratulations, sir. The S.S. think they're the first to liberate a city but they always find the Gestapo there before them. (*He salutes.*) . . . Heil Hitler!

MAN WITH FLOWER. (*Saluting, bored voice.*) Heil Hitler.

S.S. CAPTAIN. (*In German to* SOLDIERS *who have returned.*) . . . Well?

FIRST SOLDIER. (*In German.*) No one there, sir!

S.S. CAPTAIN. (*In German.*) And the cellar?

SECOND SOLDIER. (*In German.*) Empty.

COMMISSAIRE. (*Coming out of MEN'S ROOM.*) No one in here, Captain.

S.S. CAPTAIN. My apologies, gentlemen and lady. Perhaps it was my too vivid imagination that created all those voices. But why don't some of your singers accompany us down to headquarters so we may test their extraordinary vocal prowess a bit more carefully. (*In German, indicating the* TWO MEN.) . . . Take them! (SOLDIERS *seize* MEN, *pull them to their feet.*) And now my friends, goodnight.

MAN WITH FLOWER. (*As* S.S. CAPTAIN *starts out door.*) Uh, Captain. (S.S. CAPTAIN *stops. With a smile.*) . . . Heil Hitler.

S.S. CAPTAIN. (*Very conscious that he has forgotten.*) Heil Hitler! (*And he exits. The moment door is shut* MAN WITH FLOWER *starts to coat rack.*)

MAN WITH FLOWER. (*Putting on coat, starting to door.*) That meeting. The Polish Colonel and his friends. We can't have it here, this place is no longer safe. When they come, tell them I'll be at 23 Rue Macé at eight-thirty tonight. (*As he exits.*) . . . Remember, 23 Rue Macé!

CLAUDINE. (*When he is gone.*) Monsieur Clairon, where is the rabbi?

JACOBOWSKY. (*Coming out of door marked "DAMES," hatbox still in hand.*) Shalom!

PAPA CLAIRON. Lucky you thought of hiding there.

JACOBOWSKY. Not lucky. Scientific. I have learned that males, even policemen, have a reluctance to investigate a place reserved for ladies. Interesting psychologically though, did you know they write on walls too? (*To* CLAUDINE.) . . . The Colonel has not appeared yet?

CLAUDINE. A Colonel? Is he French?

JACOBOWSKY. No, Polish, but . . .

PAPA CLAIRON. We have a message for him! He is to meet his friend at 23 Rue Macé, at eight-thirty tonight.

JACOBOWSKY. (*Putting on his coat.*) There's no time to lose, would you help me find him?

CLAUDINE. I will take the road from Nantes!

PAPA CLAIRON. And I'll take the sea road. (*As he gets coat.*) . . . Who do we look for?

JACOBOWSKY. Two men, one very dignified, and a beautiful young woman. And Lulu, don't forget Lulu! Tell them S. L. Jacobowsky sent you and we meet at 23 Rue Macé, eight-thirty tonight!

(*Dark trees, bits of horse-drawn wagon, begin to appear behind them through above as* CLAIRON, CLAUDINE *and* JACOBOWSKY *exit, and we come up on . . .*

ACT TWO

SCENE 3

A PEDDLER'S WAGON stopped alongside country road. It is evening.

DRIVER. . . . What can I do, Monsieur? We have ridden for eight hours without stopping; my horse must rest or he will die.

COLONEL. But I must get to St. Nazaire, we are two hours late already!

DRIVER. I am a peddler, Monsieur, and without my horse I cannot earn my living! For me it is also life or death. (*And he crosses Upstage to his horse as* COLONEL *pounds his fist in his palm in frustration.*)

COLONEL. Man with flower, I miss him! (*In agony of self-abnegation.*) . . . Is all my fault! I hate myself! I despise myself!

MARIANNE. (*Trying to comfort him.*) Darling, you're being too harsh. What good will hating yourself do?

COLONEL. You are right. Instead of hating myself, I *do* something! I use my brain to defeat problem like that little Jacobowsky! Now if he were here, what would he do?

SZABUNIEWICZ. Probably borrow from Germans passage money to America.

COLONEL. (*Pacing excitedly.*) In every situation, no matter how dark, is always two possibilities!

MARIANNE. That's wonderful, Tadeusz! Just like Monsieur Jacobowsky!

COLONEL. The Germans, either they find the papers or they don't find the papers.

MARIANNE. Go on!

COLONEL. If they don't find the papers, that is good. But if they do find the papers . . .

MARIANNE. Yes, Tadeusz?

COLONEL. (*Trying desperately to pull the answer out of the air.*) If they do find the papers . . .

SZABUNIEWICZ. Yes, my Colonel?

COLONEL. (*It all collapses.*) That's terrible. (*In despair again.*) . . . It's no use, I do not think like Monsieur Jacobowsky!

MARIANNE. (*Gently.*) Not quite.

COLONEL. But I live like him. Hunted! I hang on to life with one hand. I live like Jacobowsky only he knows how to do it and I don't. (*As MUSIC comes up.*) . . . So much is in my head this day! Man with flower. Missing papers. Germans. But all I think about is him. (*And he sings.*)

I THINK I THINK I KNOW THE WAY IT IS
TO BE A JACOBOWSKY
I THINK I KNOW THE LONGING AND THE LONELINESS
THAT LAUGH OF HIS CONCEALS
I THINK THE THOUGHTS I THINK ARE JUST LIKE HIS
THIS LITTLE JACOBOWSKY
I TOO KNOW WHAT IT'S LIKE TO BE THE PREY
AND HAVE THE HUNTER AT MY HEELS

I TOO HAVE SMILED AT THE DANGER
PRETENDING LIFE DOESN'T HURT

I TOO HAVE DREAMED OF THE SUNLIGHT
AND HAD TO HIDE IN THE DIRT

I THINK I USED TO THINK "HOW VERY SAD
TO BE A JACOBOWSKY"
I THINK IT'S VERY FAR THAT I HAVE TRAVELED
SINCE THIS TRAVELING BEGAN
TODAY I THINK I THINK IT'S NOT SO BAD
TO BE A JACOBOWSKY
I THINK I THINK SOMEONE SO MUCH LIKE ME
MUST BE A VERY SPECIAL MAN . . .

TODAY I THINK I THINK IT'S NOT SO BAD
TO BE A JACOBOWSKY
I THINK I THINK SOMEONE SO MUCH LIKE ME
MUST BE A VERY SPECIAL MAN!

SZABUNIEWICZ. (*At end of SONG.*) . . . Colonel, someone is coming on road!

MARIANNE. Germans, we'd better hide! (*As* COLONEL *starts to road.*) . . . Tadeusz, where are you going?

COLONEL. (*As he suddenly stops, laughs.*) Szabuniewicz, Marianne, come look at your "Germans." (*And* CLAUDINE *rides by on her bicycle.*)

MARIANNE. (*As* CLAUDINE *stops, dismounts.*) Tadeusz, that was foolish! Supposing it had been a German patrol, you might have been killed.

CLAUDINE. (*Approaching* COLONEL.) Pardon, Monsieur, but I wonder if you might help me? I am looking for some friends who are perhaps lost on this road.

MARIANNE. (*Quickly.*) I am sorry, Mademoiselle, but we have seen no one. My husband and I are on our way to Bordeaux.

CLAUDINE. A party of four. Two men, a woman . . .

MARIANNE. As you see, we are three. Now if you will excuse us . . .

CLAUDINE. And Lulu.

MARIANNE. (*Stops.*) Who sent you, Mademoiselle?

CLAUDINE. A small man, a long name . . .

MARIANNE. (*Almost shouting.*) Monsieur Jacobowsky! He's found us!

CLAUDINE. That's him! I am to look for a Colonel, very dignified, that would be you, sir . . . (*She turns to* SZABUNIEWICZ, *the* COLONEL *coughs loudly.*) I beg your pardon. Your friend wishes to tell you that the meeting has been changed to 23 Rue Macé at eight-thirty tonight. (*Pushing bicycle toward him.*) Take this, I'll walk.

COLONEL. But I do not know how to negotiate this apparatus! And what about Szabuniewicz?

SZABUNIEWICZ. I catch up with you. This charming creature will show me the way . . .

COLONEL. (*As he mounts bicycle, starts walking.*) Is moving! What I do next?

MARIANNE. Pedal!

COLONEL. Pedal what?

MARIANNE/CLAUDINE/SZABUNIEWICZ. The pedals!

COLONEL. Oh. (*He begins to pedal as MUSIC of "WE'RE ALMOST THERE" comes up. He turns Right.*) . . . I am making a turn. (*Left.*) Another turn! (*Hands off handlebars.*) . . . Everybody look! I, Tadeusz Boleslav Stjerbinsky, have conquered the bicycle!

CLAUDINE. (*As COLONEL rides off Left.*) But you're going in the wrong direction!

(*MUSIC up full as bicycle reappears. MARIANNE gets on bicycle with him and both go off Right with SZABUNIEWICZ and CLAUDINE hurrying after them as PEDDLER'S WAGON disappears, and we come up on . . .*)

ACT TWO

SCENE 4

The RECEPTION ROOM OF 23 RUE MACÉ, a small Ursuline convent. At rise the SISTERS enter from their tasks as led by MOTHER MADELEINE, they sing.

MOTHER MADELEINE.
DOMINE DOMINE
CLAMAVI AD TE
EXAUDI ME
AVE MARIA IN GLORIA
AVE MARIA IN GLORIA
MOTHER MADELEINE/SISTERS.
DOMINE DOMINE

CLAMAVI AD TE
EXAUDI ME
AVE MARIA IN GLORIA
AVE MARIA IN GLORIA

(On last notes of SONG S.S. CAPTAIN *and* SIX MEN *enter Right.)*

MOTHER MADELEINE. . . . Captain, are you sure you have the right address? This is 23 Rue Macé.

S.S. CAPTAIN. Precisely. Where we shall be billeting seven men.

MOTHER MADELEINE. Captain, this is a convent, it is not possible!

S.S. CAPTAIN. Madame, this is war, everything is possible. Seven.

MOTHER MADELEINE. Sister Rolande, will you show this gentleman upstairs. There is a storeroom, not very suitable but . . .

S.S. CAPTAIN. Let me be the judge of that. We will follow you, Sister. *(There is a knock at the door.)* . . . Are you expecting visitors?

MOTHER MADELEINE. No, no, a gentleman to arrange a special mass for his wife. *(Signalling* SISTER LAURETTE *to go to the door.)* . . . Well, take the Captain upstairs, Sister Rolande. What are you waiting for? *(As* CAPTAIN *and* SOLDIERS *continue upstairs.)* And the rest of you, it's time for vespers, go along, go along!

MAN WITH FLOWER. Mother Madeleine . . .

MOTHER MADELEINE. Quiet! There are Germans in the house.

MAN WITH FLOWER. I know, I saw the cars.

MOTHER MADELEINE. They are billeting some of their soldiers here.

MAN WITH FLOWER. But my friends are due any minute!

MOTHER MADELEINE. I know, one is here already. *(There is a knock at the door.)*

MAN WITH FLOWER. Nine o'clock, that might be them!

MOTHER MADELEINE. Let me answer it, it might be more of those damn Nazis. *(To heaven as she crosses herself.)* . . . I am sorry for that. All right, I'm coming, ich kummenzie!

COLONEL. *(Coming on followed by* MARIANNE *and* SZABUNIE-WICZ.) Good evening, Reverend Mother, I am looking for man with flower . . . *(Seeing him.)* Ah, at last! May I present myself . . .

MAN WITH FLOWER. Quiet, Colonel, there are Germans upstairs!

MARIANNE. And where is Monsieur Jacobowsky?

JACOBOWSKY. *(Coming out of cellar door with hatbox.)* Dominus vobiscum! (*Handing hat to* MARIANNE.) . . . I wanted for once to see you in this little creation.

MARIANNE. My hat!

COLONEL. My papers! Szabuniewicz, child, holy motherland is saved! (*Saluting, as he takes papers from hat, presents them to* MAN WITH FLOWER.) . . . Man with flower, I Colonel Stjerbinsky hereby deliver papers for Polish government in exile!

MAN WITH FLOWER. Thank you, Colonel, but you will deliver the papers to the proper authorities when you get to England.

COLONEL. We go now?

MAN WITH FLOWER. The launch sails at ten from the old wharf on the Cap St. Jean road. I will start now and Mother Madeleine will keep you in a safe place till it's time to leave. (*As he leaves.*) . . . Ten o'clock, Colonel. One hour from now. Goodnight.

SISTER ROLANDE. (*Hurrying down the stairs.*) Mother Madeleine, the Captain says the storeroom is not large enough, he wants to know what other room we have!

MOTHER MADELEINE. Keep him there a moment, I will be up directly.

SISTER ROLANDE. I can't, he's on his way down.

MOTHER MADELEINE. Sister Rolande take our friends into the chapel, hurry! And tell the sisters they are to continue their hymns as usual.

COLONEL. (*As they start off.*) Hymns, I love hymns . . .

S.S. CAPTAIN. (*Entering at that moment.*) Three of the men will sleep up there. Now, we need room for another four.

MOTHER MADELEINE. Monsieur, as you can see we are a small order, there is only that room and the cells where the sisters sleep.

S.S. CAPTAIN. Where does that door lead?

MOTHER MADELEINE. The coal cellar.

S.S. CAPTAIN. And that passageway?

MOTHER MADELEINE. The chapel, Captain. Hardly an appropriate place for a billet. (*As S.S. CAPTAIN starts for chapel.*) . . . No! The Sisters are singing their hymns.

S.S. CAPTAIN. Madame, I am sure that God will hear them whether they are sung in the chapel or not. Now will you ask them to come out, or shall I have my men do it?

MOTHER MADELEINE. (*After a moment, calling.*) Sister Rolande, will you have the sisters come out here, please.

(*And led by* SISTER ROLANDE, *a procession of* NUNS, *their heads averted, starts out. Among the last* FOUR NUNS *we notice one who is extraordinarily tall.*)

Nuns.
DOMINE, DOMINE
CLAMAVI AD TE
EXAUDI ME
AVE MARIA IN GLORIA
 A Base Voice. (*Booming out.*)
AVE MARIA IN GLORIA
 S.S. Captain. (*As* All Nuns *kneel facing Upstage.*) Well, there was no need for you to be concerned, Madame. I am certain God would have no trouble hearing those voices wherever they were.
 Mother Madeleine. (*As* S.S. Captain *starts to last* Four Nuns *who still face Upstage.*) They *are* very unusual, the Bishop himself came all the way from Bordeaux to see them, now if you will excuse us . . .
 S.S. Captain. (*Before* Mother Madeleine *can hurry the* Nuns *away.*) I don't blame him. I'm just a tiny bit curious to see these "Sisters" myself.
 Mother Madeleine. (*As he turns round first of* Four, *who is* Marianne.) Sister Marie is a new member of our order. (*He turns round* Szabuniewicz.) . . . Sister Brigitte, very useful in the garden.
 S.S. Captain. One can see that.
 Mother Madeleine. (*As* S.S. Captain *tries to turn* Jacobowsky *who is quite reluctant.*) Sister Yvonne is a bit shy. (Jacobowsky *finally turns around with bottom part of his cowl drawn veil-like over his beard.*)
 S.S. Captain. Charming. (*Turning* Colonel *around who slowly rises to his full height.*) . . . Now for this last Sister. No, don't tell me, I know. Little Sister Bobo. Alias the clown who escaped from us in Rennes!
 Colonel. Yes, I escape from you in Rennes, but I am no clown! I am Tadeusz Boleslav Stjerbinsky, Colonel of glorious Polish Cavalry! (*Suddenly lifting* S.S. Captain *from floor and holding him as shield in front of him. To* Soldiers *who draw their pistols.*) . . . Now, you will step aside and I will lead my people out of here!
 Jacobowsky. (*Overcome with admiration.*) Moses!
 S.S. Captain. (*To* Soldiers.) Don't move! (*To* Colonel.) . . . Let me go or I will give the orders to fire!
 Colonel. Fire! To die knowing that filth like you is eliminated is to live! Shall I give the order for you? Ein, svei, drei . . .
 S.S. Captain. No! (*To* Soldiers *in German.*) . . . Lower your guns.

COLONEL. So, the master race knows fear like everyone else. (*To* SOLDIERS.) . . . Drop your pistols on the floor. (S.S. CAPTAIN *repeats his order in German.*) Now kick them over here. (*They do.*) . . . Jacobowsky, Szabuniewicz, pick up guns. (*They do.*) Where does that door lead to?

MOTHER MADELEINE. The coal cellar.

COLONEL. Szabuniewicz, please to open door. (SZABUNIEWICZ *does so.*) . . . Now, Monsieur Jacobowsky, throw them down. (JACOBOWSKY *cannot believe his ears.*) You heard me, throw them down!

(JACOBOWSKY *crosses tentatively to* FIRST SOLDIER, *smiles, nods politely, looks at him then shakes his head, he cannot do it.* MARIANNE, *still in her nun's costume, steps forward as she sings.*)

MARIANNE. (*A capella at first.*)
AT LEAST, DO IT FOR POLAND
FOR KEEPING THE FATHERLAND OUT AND THE
   MOTHERLAND FREE
(*Joined by* MOTHER MADELEINE.)
AND YOU'LL SOON EXCHANGE YOUR PALLOR
FOR THE ROSY GLOW OF VALOR
WHEN YOU DO IT FOR P-O-L-A-N-D

(JACOBOWSKY *takes a deep breath, goes to* FIRST SOLDIER, *walks him to door and almost apologetically pushes him down. He goes to* SECOND SOLDIER, *shakes his hand, dusts off his lapel and shoves him down. He begins to enjoy his work.* THIRD SOLDIER *walks over as* JACOBOWSKY *beckons him and is tripped by* JACOBOWSKY's *outstretched foot then tumbles down.*)

COLONEL. And now, we leave.

(JACOBOWSKY *signals for him to wait, goes to staircase, whistles and* FOURTH SOLDIER *comes running down.* JACOBOWSKY *gives him Nazi salute which* SOLDIER *returns and* JACOBOWSKY *goose-steps him to cellar door and kicks him down.* FIFTH SOLDIER *has come running down through this in his shirt-sleeves.* JACOBOWSKY *grabs him by his suspenders, whirls him around then pulls back elastic of suspenders and shoots him down.* NUNS *have continued singing LA LA LA through this and as* SIXTH SOLDIER *hurries down* JACOBOWSKY *takes him in his arms, dances him to cellar door, and pushes him down.*)

COLONEL. (*As* JACOBOWSKY *dusts off his hands, closes cellar door.*) Szabuniewicz, you will take Mademoiselle Marianne and wait for us outside. We will join you in a moment.

MARIANNE. Be careful, Tadeusz.

COLONEL. I will be as careful as the moment requires. (*As* SZABUNIEWICZ *and* MARIANNE *leave.*) . . . Reverend Mother, it is late. Perhaps you and the sisters would like to continue your hymns.

MOTHER MADELEINE. I think that is an excellent idea, Colonel.

S.S. CAPTAIN. (*As* MOTHER MADELEINE *and* SISTERS *start off.*) What do you mean to do now?

COLONEL. I have not yet decided.

S.S. CAPTAIN. Colonel Stjerbinsky, there are over five thousand German troops in St. Nazaire. The only sensible move is to negotiate.

COLONEL. Why should I negotiate? I am armed, you are not. I hold all the cards.

S.S. CAPTAIN. All but one. I know you, Colonel. You are a survivor from a vanished past, and your code of honor as a soldier will not permit you to shoot an unarmed man.

COLONEL. You Nazis do it.

S.S. CAPTAIN. That is different. We are not distressed by codes. We have abolished conscience and our soldiers are trained to kill without being troubled by senseless guilt. (*His voice rising through this.*) . . . But you, Colonel, *are* your code and if you break it you are nothing, you are destroyed . . . (*Suddenly, as if addressing* TWO MEN *behind the* COLONEL.) Wilhelm, Max, in here quick!

(*The* COLONEL *and* JACOBOWSKY *obey their reflexes and turn to face the unseen enemy. As they do the* S.S. CAPTAIN *bolts for the front door. The* COLONEL *swings back round just in time and shoots him. The* S.S. CAPTAIN *falls dead. There is a pause.*)

COLONEL. I have broken my code. (*Then smiling.*) . . . And it feels wonderful!

JACOBOWSKY. (*As* SZABUNIEWICZ *comes on.*) Colonel, the man with the flower said ten o'clock and that is less than half-an-hour from now!

COLONEL. Szabuniewicz, take Mademoiselle Marianne to wharf, is better we go separately. (*As* SZABUNIEWICZ *pulls* BODY OF S.S. CAPTAIN *off.*) . . . Jacobowsky, you come with me.

JACOBOWSKY. (*Shaking his head.*) It's no use, Colonel. There will
be no room for me on the boat.

COLONEL. Room is elastic, it can be made to expand!

JACOBOWSKY. I'm better off heading south while there is still
time . . .

COLONEL. (*His full Olympian authority restored.*) You are speak-
ing with one of Pilsudski's Colonels and I order you to come! From
now on I take you under my wing! Jacobowsky, child, I adopt you!

JACOBOWSKY. (*Overwhelmed.*) Oh, Colonel.

COLONEL. Call me Tadeusz.

JACOBOWSKY. Tadeusz . . .

COLONEL. (*After a moment.*) S.L. (*And he sings.*)

YOU I LIKE
SO LET ME TIP MY HAT
IN YOUR PATH
I SPREAD MY WELCOME MAT
YOU I LIKE
CAN YOU IMAGINE THAT?
ALTHOUGH YOUR WAYS MAY BE STRANGE
AND THERE'S MUCH THAT I'D CHANGE
SOMEHOW YOU I LIKE
AND WARMLY RECOMMEND
FROM NOW ON
WE'LL CALL EACH OTHER FRIEND
I'LL BE AT
YOUR SIDE UNTIL THE END
CAN YOU BELIEVE THAT I'VE FOUND
SUCH A THRILL IN THE SOUND
OF THE NEW CHORD WE STRIKE
YOU I LIKE!

(*Set begins to change from INTERIOR OF CONVENT to STREET IN
ST. NAZAIRE as* JACOBOWSKY *sings . . .*

ACT TWO

SCENE 5

JACOBOWSKY.
YOU I LIKE
SO LET ME TIP MY HAT
IN YOUR PATH

I SPREAD MY WELCOME MAT
YOU I LIKE
CAN YOU IMAGINE THAT?
ALTHOUGH YOUR WAYS MAY BE STRANGE
AND THERE'S MUCH THAT I'D CHANGE
SOMEHOW YOU I LIKE
AND WARMLY RECOMMEND
FROM NOW ON
WE'LL CALL EACH OTHER FRIEND
I'LL BE AT
YOUR SIDE UNTIL THE END
CAN YOU BELIEVE THAT I'VE FOUND
SUCH A THRILL IN THE SOUND
OF THE NEW CHORD WE STRIKE
YOU I LIKE!

(*The* TWO MEN *look at each other for a moment, then cannot resist
any longer and seizing each other by the waist they begin to
polka wildly through the EMPTY STREET. DANCE ends, applause, and they sing.*)

JACOBOWSKY/COLONEL.
YOU I LIKE
AND WARMLY RECOMMEND
FROM NOW ON
WE'LL CALL EACH OTHER FRIEND
I'LL BE AT
YOUR SIDE UNTIL THE END

(*Reprise DANCE to exit as we come up on* . . .

ACT TWO

SCENE 6

THE OLD WHARF, a few minutes later. TWO GERMAN SOLDIERS
*run past, their searchlights playing on the stone causeway lit-
tered with barrels and boxes.* SOLDIERS *exit, a moment, then*
SZABUNIEWICZ *and* MARIANNE *step out from behind a packing
case. Suddenly* SZABUNIEWICZ *turns.*

SZABUNIEWICZ. What is that?

MARIANNE. Footsteps!

SZABUNIEWICZ. (*Grabbing her hand as he draws pistol.*) Stand back!

JACOBOWSKY. (*Coming on.*) It's only me. (*Looking around.*) . . . Where's the Colonel?

MARIANNE. I thought he was with you.

JACOBOWSKY. No, we were separated by a platoon of Germans. Did you hear the new edict, it's on every radio. Because an S.S. man was killed, all aliens and Jews are to be shot on sight. (*Looking at watch.*) . . . Where is he?

SZABUNIEWICZ. Now you here guard lady, I go look for him.

JACOBOWSKY. Szabuniewicz, be careful. (*As* SZABUNIEWICZ *exits.*) . . . I wish he would get here, those patrols make me nervous.

MARIANNE. Tadeusz is a match for any German patrol.

JACOBOWSKY. (*Realizing.*) You love him, don't you.

MARIANNE. (*After a moment.*) Yes. But I'm not sure I'll marry him. Not until he learns a little of what you know.

JACOBOWSKY. (*Probing delicately to touch his fate.*) But you will always be in love with him. Of that we can be sure.

MARIANNE. (*After a moment.*) Yes, I will always be in love with him. (*This is final; the coup de grace.* JACOBOWSKY *straightens up.*) . . . But there is room in my heart also for a beloved friend. I need you both! The world needs you both!

JACOBOWSKY. (*His irrepressible humor bubbling out.*) Yes, between us we're a hero. (*They both laugh.* COLONEL *enters at that moment.*)

COLONEL. Still they are laughing! I demand to know why? (*Then sitting wearily on crate.*) . . . Forgive me, it's just that those damn Nazis are everywhere. Just now in road while they pass I have to hide in ditch like hunted animal. Now I know at last, Monsieur Jacobowsky, what it is to be you.

JACOBOWSKY. You think just because you've been lying in a ditch for five minutes you think you know what it is to be me? You'll have to lie there for centuries! And even then when you get up you will always be Colonel Tadeusz Boleslav Stjerbinsky, and when I get up, I am still S.L. Jacobowsky. The ditch follows me.

COLONEL. (*On his high horse again.*) I do not know that I care to travel with this fellow, he has a way of putting things I find most irritating. Jacobowsky, I warn you, our duel is only postponed!

JACOBOWSKY. My dear friend and opposite, our duel is for all eternity.

COLONEL. That I do not accept! I do not say we will never disagree again . . . but all eternity is too damn long!

JACOBOWSKY. (*Open-mouthed.*) My dear Colonel . . .

COLONEL. Why you look so surprised? I have always been very democratic fellow at heart but I am sometimes too shy to show it. Furthermore I am developing simply delightful sense of humor . . .

MARIANNE. (*Running into his arms.*) Oh, Tadeusz! (*As MUSIC comes up and* JACOBOWSKY *turns away.*)
I BELONG HERE
WHERE MY WORLD IS SAFE FROM HARM
YES, I BELONG HERE
ON YOUR REASSURING ARM
SO LET THE WHOLE WORLD
TRAVEL ON TO A FARAWAY STAR
BUT I BELONG HERE
I BELONG WHEREVER YOU ARE . . .

SZABUNIEWICZ. (*Running on.*) . . . Man with flower, I find him!

MAN WITH FLOWER. (*Coming on behind* SZABUNIEWICZ.) Are you ready, Colonel Stjerbinsky? The boat will be here in less than three minutes.

COLONEL. Ready, Marianne? Jacobowsky? Szabuniewicz?

MAN WITH FLOWER. I put the question to you, Colonel. This is not a group tour.

SZABUNIEWICZ. Group only three, I don't go.

COLONEL. What? You desert me?

SZABUNIEWICZ. Never! Only my heart is homesick for Poland so I go back and wait for you there.

COLONEL. Very well, but the rest of my party comes with me. You do not expect a man to leave behind his wife, do you?

MAN WITH FLOWER. All right, dammit, two places!

COLONEL. Three! Monsieur Jacobowsky comes too. I cannot leave this man here; ten steps forward is the sea, ten steps back is death . . .

JACOBOWSKY. Colonel, he is right. It's best for all of us if I leave now.

MAN WITH FLOWER. At last someone who makes sense!

MARIANNE. But what if the Germans find you?

JACOBOWSKY. Two possibilities! Either I slip through their fingers one more time . . . (*With a strange, almost eager smile.*) Or I stop and fight. (*As lights of launch appear in background.*) Now you must go, you are endangering your mission! And don't forget Lulu! (*Handing him birdcage.*) . . . And these.

COLONEL. (*Taking small box* JACOBOWSKY *gives him.*) What are they?

JACOBOWSKY. Seasick pills. I traded them for my gloves yesterday. And this is a useful phrase book, Polish/English, how to ask for your bill at the hotel, what is the price of those persimmons, very handy.

COLONEL. This man is a genius! I cannot leave him!

MAN WITH FLOWER. Come along, the boat is in. Come along!

COLONEL. (*Embracing* SZABUNIEWICZ.) Szabuniewicz, child, be careful! And tell my friends I will return as soon as I can. (*To* JACOBOWSKY.) . . . Well, my friend, between Paris and St. Nazaire we have learned a great deal about each other.

JACOBOWSKY. I have learned to admire you, Colonel.

COLONEL. And I have learned to love you, Jacobowsky. (*And he seizes him and embraces him on both cheeks as MUSIC comes softly up.* COLONEL *releases* JACOBOWSKY *and starts off to boat.*) . . . Comes, Marianne.

MARIANNE. (*To* JACOBOWSKY, *as* COLONEL *exits.*) So. Our Grand Tour is over at last.

JACOBOWSKY. No, dear lady, merely a change of conveyance and a new guide. Your Grand Tour is just beginning.

MARIANNE. And yours?

JACOBOWSKY. Continues. But with a difference. If I have found a place in the heart of a beloved friend, then what can stop me from finding my place in this world? So from now on I will no longer be running from. But going to!

MARIANNE. (*Taking his hand.*) Thank you for giving me back the Colonel.

JACOBOWSKY. Thank you for your existence. You are the light of France!

(MARIANNE *exits, and as MUSIC continues,* JACOBOWSKY *waves after her. The lights of the launch cross Upstage as he waves. The boat is quite far away when we hear* MARIANNE'S *voice over the water.*)

MARIANNE. . . . Monsieur Jacobowsky, you haven't told me what it stands for!

JACOBOWSKY. What what stands for?

MARIANNE. The S.L.!
JACOBOWSKY. The L. is just an initial.
MARIANNE. And the S.?
JACOBOWSKY. (*After a moment, with a certain pride.*) Samson!
MARIANNE. (*Her voice barely heard.*) Aah, I might have known.

(JACOBOWSKY *is alone on the wharf. He picks up his battered briefcase and sings with mounting confidence, as the set disappears.*)

JACOBOWSKY.
I'LL BE HERE TOMORROW
ALIVE AND WELL AND THRIVING
I'LL BE HERE TOMORROW
MY TALENT IS SURVIVING
IF BEFORE THE DAWN THIS FRAGILE WORLD MIGHT
    CRACK
SOMEONE'S GOTTA TRY AND PUT THE PIECES BACK
SO, FROM BENEATH THE RUBBLE
YOU'LL HEAR A LITTLE VOICE
SAY "LIFE IS WORTH THE TROUBLE"
HAVE YOU A BETTER CHOICE?
SO LET THE SKEPTICS SAY "TONIGHT WE'RE DEAD
    AND GONE"
I'LL BE HERE TOMORROW
SIMPLY GOING ON!

(*By the end of the SONG the sun has begun to rise and* JACOBOWSKY *is filled with joy as he starts toward us. The spot catches him in a FREEZE, his arms outstretched, his eyes looking hopefully to an uncertain future. A moment. Blackout. And that's the end of the show.*)

NOTE: FULL COMPANY reprise of "YOU I LIKE" as curtain
    call.

PROPERTY LIST

PROLOGUE—*In limbo*

2 suitcases
1 suitcase with rolled-up carpet, candlesticks tied to it
1 small carpet
JACOBOWSKY's briefcase

SCENE 1: SQUARE OUTSIDE HOTEL DE LA ROSE

1 round cafe table
2 cafe chairs
1 tray on table with coffee pot, cup, saucer, peach preserves, plate
   with butter, slice of Brioche, bowl of suger cubes, knife
COLONEL's *luggage, including:*
1 large trunk
1 small trunk
1 square suitcase
1 map case
binoculars in case
saber
SZABUNIEWICZ' *luggage, including:*
1 shoulder bag with comb, whisk broom, flask, guide book, toilet kit
Other Parisians carrying:
pots
bundles
satchels
food items
other personal belongings including suitcases, duffle bags, etc.
1 car *with preset gas can*
car keys
1 large Polish flag
6 small Polish flags
1 set papers for Cziesno

GERMAN CROSSOVER

4 machine guns

SCENE 2: SAINT-CYRILLE

1 birdcage with "Lulu"
4 suitcases
1 hatbox with hat
1 set of papers (same as Cziesno papers in Scene 1)
1 needle with white thread *preset in hatbox, pinned into hat lining*

SCENE 3: A LOCAL TRAIN HEADING WEST

1 fishbowl with goldfish
2 crates of chickens
Various items carried onto train including:
blankets
ironing board
radio
wicker suitcase
saws
duffle bags
hat boxes
jewelry boxes
quilt bundles
tea kettle
book bundles
guitar
zyther
bottles of wine
wicker trunk
picnic basket with plate, knife, fork, spoon, glasses, bottle with cork, table cloth, napkins
metal basket with loaves of French bread, cheeses, sausage, hard-boiled eggs
string bag with foodstuffs
hat boxes
wood tool box
horse blanket
newspapers
black briefcase
conductor's lantern
Bible
2 chickens
cheeses
various suitcases
baskets
shoulder bags
easel with painting
2 blank canvases tied together with string
playing cards
rolled rugs
silverware
roasting pan with duck

SCENE 4: WAGONS OF THE CARNIVAL MANZONI
1 sack of clothes
SCENE 5: OPEN SPOT IN THE COUNTRYSIDE NEAR RENNES
1 picnic basket with plate, knife, fork, napkin, 2 glasses, bottle with
  cork, white table cloth
3 mounds of flowers
2 duelling pistols in wood case
1 practical pistol for S.S. CAPTAIN
2 machine guns for German soldiers
SCENE 6: DRESSING AREA OF THE CARNIVAL MANZONI
1 prop costume for Hugo The Hungarian Hercules
2 rolling racks with costumes
1 table
1 large wicker trunk
1 dressing room palette with makeup preset on table
1 large wicker trunk
3 dressing stools
SCENE 7: MIDWAY OF THE CARNIVAL MANZONI
1 tuba
1 piccolo
1 trumpet
5 balloon hoops
3 clusters helium balloons on strings
cannon with fuse and dummy of JACOBOWSKY in Hugo Costume
1 long match with striker
sharpshooting board with figure of man outlined in balloons
2 loaded sharpshooting pistols on red velvet pillow
1 starter's pistol
1 whistle

ACT TWO

SCENE 1: A TREE-LINED CANAL IN THE WEST OF FRANCE
crates with vegetables
bushel baskets with vegetables
barge
SCENE 2: CAFE OF PAPA CLAIRON AT ST. NAZAIRE
6 chairs
2 tables with tablecloths
telephone
bar unit preset with:
  Talis bag with Talis, Yamulka
  ''wedding glass'' (wrapped in towel to be stepped on)

3 bottles of wine on silver tray
1 bottle cognac
24 glasses
bar towel
3 bar stools
umbrella stand with umbrellas, 2 broom handles, 2 mop handles
Katubbah
corsage
garlands of flowers
boutineers
SCENE 3: A COUNTRY ROAD NEAR ST. NAZAIRE
metal watering bucket
harness
bicycle
SCENE 4: 23 RUE MACÉ
prayer book
SCENE 5: EMPTY STREET IN ST. NAZAIRE
strings of lights
SCENE 6: THE OLD WHARF AT ST. NAZAIRE
3 pistols (non-practical)

COSTUME PLOT

PROLOGUE

JACOBOWSKY—3-piece suit, shirt, bowtie, cardigan sweater, bowler hat, suspenders

SCENE 1

MME. BOUFFIER—black lace and silk print dress with slip, wine-colored shawl

COLONEL—Military uniform with hat

SZABUNIEWICZ—Military uniform with cap

CZEISNO—jacket, vest, trousers, shirt, tie, hat, glasses

JEANNOT—shirt, vest, ties, brown trousers

CHAUFFEUR—uniform with hat

VARIOUS PARISIANS—wearing suits, sweaters, skirts, dresses, headscarves, pullovers, undershirts, etc.

GERMAN CROSSOVER

SOLDIERS—combat uniforms

SCENE 2

MME. VAUCLAIN—housedress, apron

MARIANNE—skirt, blouse, embroidered slip, hat, scarf, cardigan sweater

SCENE 3

CONDUCTOR—uniform, hat

PEASANT WOMAN—rags, worn-out sweaters, headscarves, etc.

ELEGANT LADY—feathered hat, jewelry, coat with fur collar

PASSENGERS ON TRAIN wearing various costumes from all walks of life including peasants, elegant ladies and gentlemen, workers, students, artists, clergymen, children, anything you want

SCENE 4

MME. MANZONI—handsomely-tailored equestrienne's jacket, skirt, hat

CAPTAIN MEULLER—S.S. Captain's uniform

COLONEL—jacket, baggy trousers, plaid shirt

SZABUNIEWICZ—pullover, corduroy trousers

SCENE 6

MARIANNE—gypsy costume, headdress

MADAME LILLIAN—bearded-lady costume

MME. MANZONI—tails and top hat

VARIOUS CIRCUS PERFORMERS including LION TAMER, STRONG MAN, ACROBATS, BARKERS, MUSICIANS, STILTMAN, JUGGLERS, FLAME EATERS, BELLYDANCERS, Etc.

SCENE 7

JACOBOWSKY—Hungarian Hercules costume (*Please Note: This costume must be duplicated for dummy in cannon as well as for prop costume* MADAME LILLIAN *carries on at the beginning of Scene 6*)

JACOBOWSKY—Hungarian Hercules flame cape

COLONEL—bouncing clown costume and hat (In the original production this effect was created by lining the costume with innertubes)

SZABUNIEWICZ—living-target costume (sharpshooter's assistant)

JACOBOWSKY—sharpshooter's costume

ACT TWO

SCENE 1

BARGEMAN—peasant costume

SCENE 2

CLAUDINE—dress, cardigan, hat

MOTHER OF THE BRIDE —jacket, dress, hat

FATHER OF THE BRIDE—3-piece suit, shirt, tie

BRIDE'S AUNT—print dress, hat

GROOM—dark suit, shirt, tie

BRIDE—white dress with veil

PAPA CLAIRON—vest, shirt, trousers, bar apron

MAN WITH FLOWER IN HIS LAPEL—3-piece gray suit, tie, hat

VARIOUS WEDDING GUESTS dressed in light colors for spring wedding, Yamulkas (scull caps) for men at wedding

COMMISSAIRE OF POLICE—dark suit, sweater, hat, armband

SCENE 3

PEDDLER—peasant outfit with wide-brimmed straw hat

SCENE 4

MOTHER MADELEINE and SISTERS OF CHARITY in pale-blue habits with white cowls large enough to be pulled over the face as required when JACOBOWSKY covers his beard with the cowl he's wearing

JACOBOWSKY—Nun's habit with cowl

COLONEL—Nun's habit with cowl

MARIANNE—Nun's habit with cowl

SZABUNIEWICZ—Nun's habit with cowl

SCENE 5—NOTHING

SCENE 6

MAN WITH FLOWER IN HIS LAPEL—trenchcoat